Napoleon G. Washington

The Two Princes of Baden

Volume 1

Napoleon G. Washington

The Two Princes of Baden
Volume 1

ISBN/EAN: 9783337382902

Printed in Europe, USA, Canada, Australia, Japan

Cover: Foto ©Andreas Hilbeck / pixelio.de

More available books at **www.hansebooks.com**

The Two Princes of Baden,

—OR,—

A NEW YEAR'S EVE,

AND WHAT CAME OF IT.

AN ORIGINAL DRAMA IN FOUR ACTS—WITH A PROLOGUE.

—BY—

NAPOLEON 'G. WASHINGTON, Esq.

"The frigid and unfeeling thrive the best;
And a warm heart in this cold world is like
A beacon light, wasting its feeble flame
Upon the wintry deep that feels it not."

Entered according to Act of Congress in the year 1880, by NAPOLEON 'G. WASHINGTON, in the office
of the Librarian of Congress at Washington.

NEW YORK:
PHIL. COWEN, PRINTER,
498–500 Third Ave.

Dec. 8th, 1880.

To my

Dear Father—Sister and Brothers,

in Heaven,

And my Darling Mother on Earth,

I Lovingly Dedicate

This Work.

PRINTER'S PREFACE.

In preparing the work of Napoleon G. Washington for press, we have been struck with the manner in which he has woven the scheme and shaded the plot of the play·

There is no common grouping together of characters and scenes. The work is begun boldly and grandly, and finished in the same lofty fashion. The effort is filled with sparkling wit. It is equally balanced between the sombre and the merry. Besides, everything has been so precisely explained by the Author, that there's nothing left either for the stage manager or the actor to do but to go ahead and follow instructions.

A part of the plot of the play was taken from "The Watchman," a German tale; and so rigidly has the author held to it (when forming that part which embraces this section), that to a careless reader it might appear that some of the colloquial parts had been utilized; yet comparison would plainly shew that this s not the case. There might be such a thing as a similarity between some few verses (in the above-mentioned section)—mere connecting points. But we do not see it. Yet, if it be so, it matters not a trifle, as such as this is of no material consequence.

We have said that part of the plot was founded on a German tale, but upon further investigation we almost feel this an incorrect statement ; for to speak frankly, the author has handled so neatly the story, blended so elegantly the original with the meagre old plot, that we deem it our duty to say that the plot is almost as original as the beautiful language this noble work contains—language that would do honor to a Bulwer, a Macaulay, or a Gov. Henry.

> Great Britain boasts a Shakespeare,
> France a Moliere,
> And we hope America will rejoice
> In a Washington ?

'Tis true, she already rejoices in a Washington—a dear old President, whom Lafayette styled, " a God-like chieftain, and who, strange to say, is an ancestor of our author. But we do not mean this type of Wa hington, we mean a literary gi nt—a genius of the pen.

Gentle Public :—As we close our Preface, we imagine we hear your hearty voices echoing these, our latest thoughts. May honors fall upon the deserving head of our friend, the author; may he spared a long life: and may he spend that life in producing for our pleasure and edification many more such beautiful plays.

N. B. The author has not only shown himself master of his mother-tongue, but also master of the stage business.

AUTHOR'S PREFACE.

In placing this work before the public, I do so not with that feeling of pride usually accompanying a literary effort of any importance. I merely offer it to my friends, the good citizens of New York (and all other cities), as something which I hope will contribute to their general amusemen:.

There is no one better aware than myself of the impossibility of suiting all. Yet, at the risk of being considered vain, I entertain the hope that my production will wind itself around the hearts not only of my countrymen, bu: also my brothers and sisters, who claim the sunny soil of distant lands as their home.

Of course, I am desirous that my work shall triumph pecuniarily. But I am content if I obtain the good opinion of thoughtful men and women.

I salute you,

NAPOLEON 'G. WASHINGTON.

New York, U. S. A., August 15th, 1880.

CHARACTERS, ETC.

PROLOGUE.

Spirit of Drama............ ....*A Histrionic Goddess.*

PLAY.

Catherine Montagna, ⎫
Gottlieb Montagna, ⎭ ....*Yeomen*

Philip Montagna....................................,,*Son of Catherine and Gottlieb*

Rose Marbury.....................................*A Peasant Girl Betrothed to Philip*

Widow Marbury...*Mother of Rose*

Prince Julien.. ,.............*Son of the Margrave*

Baron Von Dietz.. ....*Minister of Finance*

Baroness Von Dietz..........................*Wife to the Minister of Finance*

Sir Abraham Levi..............................., ...*Kn't and Money-Lender*

Paddy York........ ....,...*An Irishman—A man that would die for Science*

Prof. Wiseman ....*A Teacher of the Science of Fossilology*

First Citizen.............................. ....*A Yeoman*

Second Citizen............... ...."

Lieutenant Broadsword...................*An Officer—A Soldier—And a Gentleman*

Village Girl...*The Daughter of a Yeoman*

Third Citizen..*A Yeoman*

Count Wortenburgh..*Lord High Chamberlain*

A Servant... ....*To the Chamberlain*

Princess de Albeaux.......................*A French Lady Beloved by the Chamberlain*

General Harold de Baldwin.......... ....*A Saxon Field-Marshal*

Lady De Baldwin..*Wife of the Field-Officer*

Col. Bloomingdale..........................*An Artillery Officer of the Grand Army*

Baron Stamwitz....... ....*Treasurer of Baden*

Henrique Moritz..............................*Confidential Page to Prince Julien*

Prince Herman.......................*Duke of Chemnitz—Father of Gen. De Baldwin*

Lieutenant Reber....................... ....*An Officer of Police*

Two Sentinels ....*Belonging to the Police Department*

First Gen D'Arme.. ....*Police*

First Watchman............... ...."

Capt. Wetzelburgh........... ....*Deputy Chief of Staff to the Chief of Police*

Col. Del Buchardo.............................*A Spanish Officer traveling in Baden*

Duke Von Brunswick............... ....*Chief of Police*

Second Gen D'Arme................... ....,*Police*

Second Watchman.."

A Corporal of Gen D'Armes................................ ....,...............,"

Ida Stover ⎫
Florence Stover ⎭ *Florence, Mother to Ida, and wife of Leopold the Florist.* *Yeomen.*

Miriam Isaacs ....*A Jewish Peasant Girl—Friend to Florence*

Sergeant Seldner........... .. ..*A Regular of the Reserves*

Capt. Sir Emil Valdmeyer............*An Officer of the Grand Army, and the richest and the basest Nobleman in Baden, First loved and then hated by Miriam*

Lieut. Sir Albert Josephthal.....................*An Officer serving under Valdmeyer*

Cadwallader..*Abbot of Convent of Holy Cross*

Brother Andrew...*Secretary of Convent*

Grand Judge ....*An Exiled Spanish Prince, Stern in the Law*

Leopold Stover...............................*A Florist—Husband to Florence—a Yeoman*

Wiseacre..*Jester to the Margrave, in love with Pauline*

Pauline..........................*Maid to the Princess Louise, in Love with Wiseacre*

Lord High Coroner...*A Mild Old Gentleman*

Lord Youth ....*A Vealy Young Man—A sort of Jack-a-dandy*

Grand Commissioner...............*A Lordly Bully (that is, when backed by Power)*

Ethelbert, "The Just "..*Margrave of Baden*

Vallenstern..*Chancellor of Baden (Greatly Prized by the Margrave.)—A Self-Made Man—Uncle to Miriam.*

Dr. Stern...*A Learned Chemist*

Princess Louisa............*Niece to the Margrave—in Love with Prince Julien*

Courtiers—Citizens—Soldiers—Priests—Gens D'Armes—Police Proper—Watchmen and Masqueraders representing all sorts of personages.

A Hint at Costumes, and Scenic Plot.

C O S T U M E S.

Count Wortenbergh dresses as a Brahmin. Prince Heiman as a Sultan. General De Baldwin as a Chinese Mandarin and the Princess De Albeaux as a Carmelite. Lady De Baldwin in the fashion of a gay widow of the period. Philip appears in court in court dress, minus a coronet and rapier. The Yeoman (who are considered a grade above the pea antry) dress richer, the females wearing longer skirts than peasant maids. Military men and police of all branches.—Courtiers and nobles, of whatsoever rank, all dress in strict conformity with the style of the time. · At court, the nobility appear with coronets, every male person wearing a rapier, holding the degree of gentleman.

SCENIC PLOT.

1ST ACT.

Scene 1st in 4—Closed in—Tormenters—Interior of Cottage.

   "   2d "   1—Exterior—Street.

   "   3d "   3—Exterior (Semi-Suburban)—Street.

   "   4th Full Stage—Exterior of Palace—Street.

   "   5th in 2—Interior of Cottage—Street.

   "   6th—Full Stage—(Public Square)—Exterior.

2D ACT.

Scene 1st in 1—(Facade and gable of Palace with high wall and trees)—Exterior—Street.

   "   2d   —Full Stage—Closed in—Borders or Roof—Tormentors—Interior of Palace.

   "   3d "   1—Exterior—Street.

3RD ACT.

Scene 1st in 2—Closed in—Tormentors—Interior of (Citadel or) Town's Castle.
 "   2d " 1—Exterior—Street.
 "   3d   —Full Stage—Exterior of Cathedral—Street.
 "   4th " 1—Exterior of Convent—Rear—Country.
 "   5th " 1—Facade and gable of Convent—Country.
 "   6th " 4—(Same as first in first Act.)

4TH ACT.

Scene 1st in 1—Tormentors—Interior of Palace—Antechamber.
 "   2d " 1—   "   "   " —A Hall.
 "   3d   —Full Stage—Closed in—Borders or Roof—Tormentors—Interior of Audience Chamber of Palace.

A SYNOPTICAL SCHEDULE OF STAGE DIRECTIONS, ETC.

C, means   Centre.   C. D. means Centre Door.
R. C. " Right "   D. R. C. " Door Right Centre.
L. C. " Left   "   D. L. C " " Left   "
R.   " Right   C. A. " Centre Arch.
L.   " Left   A. R. C. " Arch Right Centre.
                A. L. C. means Arch Left Centre.

Tor. means Tormentors—F. means Flats—W. means Wings.
P. S. means Prompt Side (is always so spoken) and is the right side of stage.
O. P. Side means Opposite Prompt Side, and is the left hand of stage.
Scenarium " the entire stage from top to bottom.
Proscenium " all that part of the theatre wall each side and over the arch where the scenic curtain raises and lowers.
R. I. E. means Right first entrance. L. I. E. means Left first Entrance, etc., etc. The two last entrances are styled R. U. E. and L. U. E , meaning Right Upper and Left Upper Entrances. Vampires are mechanical contrivances so arranged in the flats or wings as to make it appear that the person or persons who are called upon to use them have the power to disappear into or through any substance. Traps are situated on the floor of the stage, and are identical with vampires.

EXPLANATION OF THE ARRANGEMENT OF THE CAST.

It will be observed that I have arranged the cast in this play in a manner never yet seen by the public. But, that the public will like it much better than the old and occult style, I am convinced. The following contains my reasons :
    If a Play contained a number of characters, and was written in any sort of lofty style, I noticed that the persons performing therein were not clearly made out; that is, they would have to do a deal of strutting and chaffing before the audience really discovered who they were, and what relation they bore to the play. Now, my method entirely obviates all this annoyance; for I have arranged it so that, as the play progresses, the characters come forward as they are billed, which is strictly in rotation in the course of the story, thus beginning and ending the tale on the programme as it begins and ends in the book.
    This method is much clearer than the old manner, and enables even a child to keep a run of the play in every particular. In fact, to be brief and honest, I can not see the sense in arranging the characters of a drama in the old clumsy manner I have just described.
    The manner in which I have first introduced my characters in my book, is also an original plan, and helps an actor or an actress to immediately discover where their part begins, without looking the play through. The handiness of this feature will not only be readily detected by the profession, but by all who read this work.
    I will also mention, for the edification of the public, that the date of this play is the early part of the 17th century.

                                                    AUTHOR.

    N. B.—All instructions, directions, elucidations, etc., embracing the stage, are from the pen of the author.

PROLOGUE.

SPIRIT.—[Bowing.]
Dear friends, with all my heart I give ye greeting,
And as time is fleeting and we've much to do,
My speech shall be a mere preamble,
Enough to make our plot just plain to you.
The opening scene is in a Cottage,
Where dwells stern worth in all its sterling parts,
An upright son—a father and mother noble ;
In fact a trio of honest hearts.
In another cottage a peasant maid resides,
Pure as the angels that live above,
The daughter of a soldier's widow,
With her this son is deep—aye, mad in love.
A Jewess, wronged by a miscreant knight,
Who dies by the self same woman's hand ;
An Abbot and Monks, whose deeds, are bright
As the noonday's sun when smiling on the land ;
A Judge and Commissioner, stern and haughty ;
A Coroner, mild and gentle as a child ;
A wayward Prince, too fond of sparking,
Who upturns the city, setting the authorities wild ;
A husband and wife who've long been severed,
A little girl belonging to the two,
Unite again, forming a happy family,
A sacred scene — a picture fair to view.
A Margrave, Chamberlain, Ushers and Soldiers,
A crowd of courtiers, some robbers of the state ;
A lofty Chancellor of great experience,
Who finds in the Jewess his niece—also his fate ;
A bold Lieutenant with comely figure,
A man in whom a nation should delight,
Wins the esteem of his august Sovereign,
And a place at Court of goodly trust and might ;
A loyal Sergeant—a Chemist learned,
A lass in love with a fool that's wise :
A jester of perspicacity,
A man much noted for his sharp replies.
A host of other goodly characters,
Correct and meet all in our effort wrought,

The base are punished, the true rewarded,
A lesson to both old and young is taught.

(Suddenly after looking R.)

The chief of the Scenarium, now to me beckons,
Which means come. Thou hast had too much to say,
So now, my friends, with kisses I leave thee,
That ye may feast thine eyes upon our proper play.

Bows. Exits R. Music until Flats are thoroughiy opened and
fully reveal the cottage of the Montagnas.

ACT FIRST.—SCENE FIRST.

Scene.—Interior of a cottage, a table L. C., on which is an open book
and a lighted lamp, two high-backed easy-chairs of an ancient type, beside
table oppositely placed ; pictures on walls, several ordinary chairs of a suitable
kind, a high-backed settee R. A., lofty antique fire-place and a mantel L., on
which (the mantel) are some quaint ornaments. A bright fire is visible on the
hearth. A tall clock C., against back-scene formed by flats, D. R. C. Window with curtains and outside shu:ters L. C. Catherine and Gottlieb discovered, Catherine looking out of window, Gottlieb seated beside table nearest fire,
smoking a pipe and toying with his staff.

CATHARINE MONTAGNA [*Closing Window*]. —
Gottlieb, my husband, stay in the house to-night ; let
Philip take thy place and watch for thee. It's snowing
again, and extremely cold ; in fact the weather's too se
vere for thee to go forth ; thou knowest too well it will
effect thy wounds—ah, thy wounds! the mentioning of
them causes my mind to revert to the period—the
dreadful battle where thou didst receive them ; oh,
what a cruel thing is war; those who have not the
slightest grudge 'gainst the other, are forced by it to
meet in deadly encounter, to wres'le, as it were, for
one other's lives—in fact to commit murder; to make
orphans and create widows. Murder it may not be
termed, yet it is the same crime under a more honorable cognomen. If war was only undertaken as the
dernier resort of outraged justice, or for liberty's sake,
or as a lesson to tyrants, there would be then (bloody
as it is) some purpose in it, and scars gained therein
would be sacred as a Serapoli's raiment. But as it is,
at the will, through the machinations and for the per-
petuation of despots most generally, it is thus most
cruel. For in this case the chief object is that a few
men's names be engraved on stone, and sounded by
the brazen trump of fame throughout the world.

GOTTLIEB MONTAGNA.—Well, thou art quite right in some respects, Catherine, but—though our country's a Monarchy and our Sovereign's therefore a hereditary ruler, he is a most worthy man, and means well. If he were but cognizant of the dishonest doings of some of the officers of State, I'm sure he'd against them most rigidly wage war. His liege favors the people and good government, Catherine. When ye speak of my wounds thou dost cause mineself to recur to that eventful time when to me they were bequeathed; when my bold comrades died like Homeric heroes, and our valiant foe yielded up the ghost with equal bravery. Ensanguined as is the field of battle, yet doth my heart beat high, and a feeling of pride course through my veins as I think of my part of that memorable period. 'Twas I who did the rampart first mount, and our banner unfurl on the staff where so proudly had floated the ensign of our enemy. I struck down the hand of that lion-hearted commander of the garrison as he was in the act of applying a burning brand to the magazine. He seemed to prefer death rather than live to surrender up his sword—a soldier's sceptre. Yet it was I that made him prisoner, and who was the instrument of causing that victory to be worth its costly purchase; for had the chief of our opponents succeeded, it would have been (from the position of things), a death-blow to our cause instead of it being, as it was, the nucleus around which gathered peace and a happy conclusion of our arms.

CATHERINE.—A very happy conclusion for thee, I must confess. The officer who led—or rather the popinjay who followed the charge gained promotion and the spurs of knighthood—gained, said I? I meant were gained for him (which, I suppose, were no new thing), while Sergeant Montagna, the real hero who, being through his injuries no longer fit for the active duties of the camp, was pensioned off with the dignified station of city-watchman at a starving salary—a happy conclusion, truly; never even spoken of in the dispatches of the puppy, who commanded the troops to which thou didst belong.

GOTTLIEB.—Captain Nidig was a mean man, 'tis true, and never deserved the spurs, yet there's consolation in knowing that our country profited by the success of our armies, and a satisfaction in being aware

that the guards to which I belonged brave in action
proved themselves. I am surprised at thy seeming want
of patriotism, Catherine ; thou who hast always been
so loyal. How comes it that ye talk in this fashion—
the daughter of a soldier, too—thy conversation hath
generally been marked for deep thought, and though
thou hast, (as I have already admitted), said some
truths, yet thou art surely not thyself ; I am afraid the
insufficiency of our purse to procure the luxuries of
grandees annoys thee too much. Let us be thankful
that we have never wanted for a meal, and that we still
have our dear boy Philip to love, and that he cherishes
us in return. Be less proud and thou'll be more con-
tented ; if good fortune be in store for us, believe me
it will overtake us just as sure as that the sun will appear upon the morn. The same with misfortune—the
ways of Providence are inscrutable and unalterable.

[Enter Philip doffing hat, from D. in F. R. C.].

PHILIP MONTAGNA —A busy night, this, a very
busy night.

CATHERINE.—Philip, thou hast arrived in proper
time—right in season, lad ; I was just speaking about
thee ; thou'll have to watch for thy father to-night, for
surely it will never do for him to go on duty—it's too
severely cold ; besides, there's every indicative that the
present storm will be a bitter one ; yes, my son, I prog-
nasticate a deep fall of snow.

GOTTLIEB. [*Putting aside pipe*].—Ah, Philip; thy
father's not what he once was, but, though my wounded leg troubles me more than usual, if it were not that
I had at present an attack of rheumatism, I could get
along, for I've stood many a night as cold as this on
guard; a fall of snow would not bother an old warrior,
a veteran of five pitched battles ; no, no ; I'd laugh at
the snow, my boy; but this rheumatism is a terror. I'm
sorry my lad, but—

PHILIP. [*Taking his father's hand*].—Dear Father, thou dost wrong me is thou dost think that doing
thee so slight a service can annoy me ; I have not forgotten the many sacrifices thou hast made for myself.
It was for the taking of thy place on the watch to-night
that brought me here so early ; my employer, (kind
heart that he is), sends thee this as a New Year's gift
[*puts a purse in Gottlieb's hand*], as a token ; he says of

his remembrance of the many kindnesses rendered by
thyself to him when he needed assistance.

GOTTLIEB. [*Counting money*].—Why this, my
son, is indeed a New Year's present—seventy-five rix-
dollars. Why, this sum seems almost like a small fortune.

CATHERINE.—Philip, the time was when thy father
was a well-to-do confectioner   It wears the color of a
dream now, more than a reality. I thank Leopold for
his token of regard and kind remembrance   Yet, it
casts a melancholy shadow whose gloomy presence dis-
sipates the pleasure lodged in the gift. When I think
we once were dispensers instead of recipients of chari-
ty; many besides Leopold hath partaken of our bounty.

GOTTLIEB.—Hold, my good wife ; Leopold remem-
bers this, and, like a sincere friend, (being again quite
comfortable), wishes to let us understand it, and to render us in the mean time a little pleasure by showing
that though money and success may take wings, a true
friend always remains the same; would there were more
cast in his mould. But of all our acquaintances he
alone holds steadfast ; I shall drink his health and to
the success of all his undertakings to-morrow in a bottle of Burgundy.

PHILIP. *Taking his mother's hand*].—Cheer up,
mother, remember that I have always looked upon thee
as philosopher ; discredit not thy title ; hath not thine
own tongue proclaimed that poverty was no disgrace ?
Surely the sun of prosperity will again smile upon our
house and gladden our hearts.

CATHARINE. [*Embracing Philip*].- I hope so,
my son, I do, indeed. Yet certainly thou art aware
that the most sanguine temperament or the most zealous
person will at times despair; when fate seems constantly to wear a nebulous contour ; at this climax one
quite loses patriotism, becoming warped, as it were, almost feeling that all things are a mockery, appearing
disloyal to heaven and militant with nature.

GOTTLIEB.—My dear Catherine, I'm very much
afraid that at our New Year's feast a bad companion
thou art going to prove us ; if I could only persuade
thee to follow my plan of taking a little wine now and
then, much of thy misery wouldst thou escape ; a misery, it seems, thy fretful mind (for I fear, me, 'tis so

grown), is now heir to ; but, dear wife, let's change the subject to something more pleasant to our Philip's ears. [*Turning to Philip*]. My Son, how is little Rose, and how is her mother ? Hast thou seen thy sweetheart lately ? But pshaw ! that's a question most useless, for thou hast certainly beheld her many times since last Sabbath. Have they succeeded in their new venture ?

PHILIP.—Very well ; better than they could have anticipated under the circumstances, for thou dost remember that when Rose's father died. her mother and herself became involved in one difficulty after another, until they were forced to mortgage their cottage. But the little school which they have lately inaugurated, Rose hopes will be the means not only of liquidating the claim of the mortgagee, but leave them a fair compensation besides. Rose teaches the older scholars, while her mother presides over the ' Kinder-Garten." Rose and her mother bade me say that they were coming to spend the day. and dine with us on the morrow. Good Leopold told me to inform thee that he would have business that would bring him in the vicinity of our house this evening, and that he should claim its hospitality for the night, and be happy to make one of the number at our New Year's dinner. Father, [*takes two parcels from coat-pocket*] though I'm no apologist or disciple of smoking, yet, knowing that thou dost like the " weed " to enjoy. I do present thee with this Hamburg pipe. Here's [*turning to Catherine*], something for mother, too, in the way of a pair of ear-rings and breast-pin. I wish I were only able, my dear parents, to present ye both with tokens more befitting the love I bear thee.

[Gottlieb and Catherine both examine their presents, looking exceedingly pleased].

GOTTLIEB. [*With emotion*].—P-h-i-l-i-p—ahem, t-h-o-u a-r-t a g-o-o-d b-o-y. W-i-f-e, w-h-a-t-'-s t-h-e m-a-t-t-e-r w-i-t-h t-h-e fi-r-e, s-u-r-e-ly i-t s-m-o-k-e-s, I f-e-e-l m-y e y-e-s s-m-a-r-t a-s i-f, ahem, P-h-i-l-i-p, t-h-i-s i-s a fi-n-e p-i-p-e.

CATHERINE.—My dear, dear son, thou art the delight of our old age. May heaven reward thee, I can give thee nothing better in return for your kindness than a mother's fondness, a mother's prayer—a prayer that thy heart shall always be pure, and true, as it now is ; possessing a clear conscience, ye will be rich—

rich in a wealth that counts on high ; 'tis a gem out-balancing in value the showy pomp of sceptered prin-ces.

GOTTLIEB.—Philip, if thou hadst been like some sons, saved thy money for thyself, thou might have married Rose this many a day ; but take comfort, lad, we are old and feeble, thou'll not have to be troubled with us a great while longer. Out of nine children thou art the youngest, and the only survivor ; and thou —now thirty summers do reckon by the calendar—sure-ly the sands of our lives must be nearly run when the baby hath encompassed this cycle.

PHILIP.—Father, what art thou talking of ? Rose is dear—yes, dearer than my life But I'd give up this priceless jewel were she a hundred times as dear, rather than desert thee and my darling mother. I prithee think not for one moment that I could be as bare as to desire the abbreviation of thy lives by hoary headed Time ; much as I love Rose, the hour that takes my parents from this earth will be to me most sad.

CATHERINE.—Thou art right, Philip, loving and marrying are not in the Holy Commandments, but to honor thy father and mother is a sacred duty enjoined on thee by the Supreme Being. But Rose—how does she entertain this long waiting ?

PHILIP.—Take no thought of Rose on that particu-lar point, for she will be but twenty on the fifteenth of next March. Ye remember by the Romans called the " Ides," (the day on which great Cæsar yielded up his lofty soul), she can well afford to wait, thou dost per-ceive, especially when she loves me and knows that her affection is reciprocated ; when she is fully aware that I idolize her. Rose hath sworn to wed no man but me, not if he were a belted Knight, or heir to the throne of the Margrave. But come, tell us what thou dost intend to have in the way of eatables for the morrow's feast.

CATHERINE.—Well, let me see—boiled venison, fried fish, a little pig roasted, with plenty of dressing ; par-snips, turnips mashed in milk, pickled tongue and on-ions, and a bouquet of flowers for ornament. Ah ! I forgot to mention bread, butter, rolls and doughnuts. This I think is a very—or rather will make quite a com-fortable meal. Cider and apples, too, with cracked nuts for desert. Philip, 'tis because thou art so good a son that we are enabled on the morrow to set so plentiful a table, and—

GOTTLIEB.—Don't forget the Burgundy. An entertainment without Burgundy is no entertainment. The best I ever remember having tasted, was some rare old stuff, presented to Stover just about the time of his marriage with Florence Steinberg. Poor Leopold, he did not long enjoy conjugal felicity. Yet I can never bring myself to think that Florenee and Parson von Beecherton eloped. Its too dreadful to be credited.

CATHERINE.—Yes, Gottlieb, that was a sad affair. But though I do believe they did elope, yet am I of the opinion that that handsome insinuating housekeeper, Lydia Brutzan, who abided with them then, was at the bottom of, and the cause of, all the mischief, that befel Leopold and Florence.

PHILIP.—The Parson was a disgrace to his cloth.

GOTTLIEB.—To contemplate thus, were to think too dismally. Beecherton was a minister. I cannot couple such a crime, with such a calling. 'Tis said, he was an ill-behaving man, I'll admit; but such a deed as this—Oh, no; 'tis too terrible.

PHILIP —Father, set not so great a store on calling,—'tis not that which makes the man; no, not even in religion. The wearers of sacred gowns are but men, and according as they are base or virtuous, so shapes the faith. Too often religion is assumed the surer to veil dark purposes, or a greedy thirst for power; better backed by the superstitions of over zealous and too credulous satellites. Yet there are those on whom the sacerdotal robes do fall; whose lives are hallowed, and whose works of goodness o'ershadow the land; who teach the creed of the Holy Nazarene after his own fashion (divested of all that pageantry and mummery utilized to awe petty and unthinking minds, mere chicanery which has for its birthplace the brain of ambitious churchmen)· These true disciples elevate their calling, though that be to preach the Gospel. For the faith may be perverted, but they can never be. Father, immeasurable as is the difference, yet remember, a just man takes rank after the Deity:

CATHERINE.—Philip, an orator art thou.

GOTTLIEB.—Philip, thou art a wise boy; and if thy

mother and I avoid the summons of the Death-Angel a little while longer, we shall behold thee a great man.

PHILIP.—If I did not know it were my dear parents who spoke thus, I might attach unto myself a consequence undue. I greatly fear that the fervor of thy love blinds thee both to my imperfections.

GOTTLIEB.—Well, my son, thou hast few imperfections; yet I'll not attempt to debate with thee upon the subject; but there's one thing I will say, and that is, I will hold thee to account if on the morrow the Burgundy does not grace our festal boards.

PHILIP.—Never fear, father, thou shalt have Burgundy on the morrow; I promise thee I shall see to it myself. I—

CATHERINE.—Nay, Philip, I spread the cloth, and we'll partake of supper first, and then—

PHILIP.—I have supped with Leopold. Mother, I shall be back in a few minutes Have father's staff, horn, and great-coat ready, please when I return; as for the watch, it will be more of a pastime than a hardship tonight, as there will be a considerable amount of merriment going on outside. From the appearance of things, masqueraders will do a lively business.

SECOND SCENE.

Scene.— A street (front prospective).—Enter Rose and Widow Marbury L, arm-in-arm

ROSE MARBURY.—O, what a lovely night. I am so glad the snow has stopped falling. Dear mother, thou needst not accompany any further, it'll be but a few steps to Matilda's from here· Lonely I shall not feel, there are so many out.

WIDOW MARBURY.—As ye wish, my child But who at Matilda's are invited to bring in the year?

ROSE.—Only a few young people who dwell hard by. Philip, of course, was invited, along with myself. But, as he informs me (by message) he must watch tonight for his father, it will be impossible for him to attend.

WID. MAR.—Then I suppose Maurice Minzesheimer (Matilda's chosen one), will escort thee home. Well, Philip will make no objections to this, feeling he hath naught to fear from an engaged young man. Besides he holds Maurice in high favor·

ROSE —It will not be necessary to trouble Maurice, as Philip has arranged it (so he says in his note), with Corporal Vollensdorf, so that he will be relieved in time to escort me home. The Corporal will dismiss him just after midnight, one square from the Cathedral of St. Gregory, where thou know'st we are to meet. I'm to follow him until he is relieved, after which on his dear stout arm I am to lean, and—

WID. MAR.—[Laughingly] Like two turtle doves walk home.

ROSE.—Thou hast said mother, O, how proud I feel when I think that I, Rose Marbury, a poor peasant girl, have won the love of such a splendid man as Philip Montagna. Well, mother, we must part now, or I shall be late at the gathering.

[Rose and her mother en brace and kiss].
[Exit. Widow L. Rose. R.]

THIRD SCENE.

Scene.—A semi-suburban view. Enter L, Philip as bell tolls the hour of ten.

PHILIP.—[With horn.] Toot-toot-tu, toot-toot-tu, toot-toot-tu. [Calls] Ten o'clock, and all is well. [Sings]:
Ye are warned of the hour by the loud-throated bell,
But it's only the watchman knoweth all is well. [horn]
Toot-toot-tu, Toot-toot-tu, Toot-toot-tu. Thank goodness, the time speeds so quickly by; soon my darling Rose shall—

[Enter Prince Julien R.]

PRINCE JUL.—I've caught thee at last, my lad, and right glad I am sir. How thou has eluded me so long, I cannot understand. I've been following thee for nearly half an hour, yet have not been able to gain thy side until this present moment.

PHILIP.—Well, what wouldst thou with me. I know thee not.

PRINCE JUL.—Strange would it be if thou shouldst know me, masked as I am.

PHILIP.—The full intent of my words ye take not. Know 'tis the duty of a city watchman to recognize neither friend or foe when on guard at night. unless the foe be not personal, but an enemy of the State's good laws. Recognizance in this case means arrest; a friend can only be recognized if he has something of moment ◂to impart. The law covers masked or unmasked persons, I have said, and it will be well for thee to weigh thy speech.

PRINCE JUL.—That will be impossible, Sir Watchman, as I have not at hand the required scales.

PHILIP.—Thy facetiousness, Sir Mark, may procure for thee the guard house. Know that when ye mock at me ; thou dost affront the statutes.

PRINCE JUL.—A truce with thy severity; good friend, and list ye a moment to what I shalt say. It will be as much of a surprise to thee as were the contents of the " Wonder Box" to Pandora. Now pick up thine ears. Thou art a city watchman. Well—

PHILIP.—I at least wear the uniform, and act in the capacity of such, for the time be.ng.

PRINCE JUL.—Well, what I propose is, that we exchange places and garments for the remainder of thy watch, re-exchanging at the great entrance of " St. Gregory's " at a trifle before midnight.

PHILIP.—[Looking amazed.] What art thou driving at ? surely thou hast been hobnobbing with Backus. Why man if I were to engage in this nonsense with thee, naught but trouble to both of us would come of it.

[Philip essays to leave, but is grasped by the arm by the Prince and detained].

PRINCE JUL.—Stop, good guardian of the peace, I swear on the honor of a gentleman that nothing detrimental to thee or thine shalt happen. If thou wilt but grant my request I promise thee a rich reward. Come, now, thou art a jolly fellow and won't refuse me ; I· like thy face. I do, indeed.

PHILIP —[Aside.] I'm half inclined to let this man have his way. [Shivers.] This is the coldest night I've ever experienced. 'Twill be unwatchmanlike, I know, but oh how nice it would be to thaw myself in some cosey tavern over a pot of sparkling beer.— [Aloud.] What if I should grant thy request ?

PRINCE JUL.—I'll vote thee a gentleman, and I'll double the reward that I was going to bestow on thee ; give me the circumference of thy " beat" and lets proceed to business.

PHILIP.—Knoweth thou the duties of a watchman ?

PRINCE JUL.—I rather think I do, but if I should

make a misstep be assured that (as I have already told thee) no harm shalt befall thee or thine. That I will keep my oath and have power to back my word.

PHILIP.—[Aside.] Some gentleman of the Court desirous to have a bit of a lark. I'll warrant. [Aloud.] This is the Eastern District, my "beat" takes in the "Boulevard" to "St. Gregory's" and a square on either side: prove to me that thy knowledge of this watch is not pretended, and I'm thine to command.

PRINCE JUL.—[Slapping Philip on back] Good, I knew thou wouldst turn up a trump. Now mark me. The business of a city watchman is to carefully patrol his "beat" and keep order. If he thinks it necessary he may at any time call to his aid the Gen d'Armes. He must call the hour, etc. after the tolling of the district bell, so as to show that he is faithfully attending to his duty. There are twenty three watchmen in each district, one of them a sargeant and two of them corporals. Now——

PHILIP —That will do, I'm satisfied, ye seem like a man of principle, and I think I may safely trust thee ; let's exchange now as speedily as possible lest peradventure we be interupted.

'The Prince now takes Philip's great-coat, hat, horn and staff, and Philip receives the Prince's sword, hat, cloak and mask. Both done hastily.'

PRINCE JUL.—Comrade, here's something to procure entertainment with [hands Philip some banknotes] while I play watchman. When we exchange at "St. Gregory's ," I'll see that thou hast a "tip" worth all thy risk.

PHILIP.—[Putting aside money.] Thanks good sir—I do not mind it. Had I not better stop with thee till the next calling, so as to make surety double sure.

PRINCE JUL. (Replacing money.) No. There's no need, I'm quite a musician and well acquainted with the watch-song, cry and horn blast. Having marked them so often. Why I'm a thorough watchman.

PHILIP.—But sir, may be - ——

PRINCE JUL.—May bees fly not this season of the year Off with thee this moment, or I'll put thee in the "Cage," off I say or I'll lock thee up. Pretty fellow, proffering instruction to a watchman (Shakes staff.) Off—away this instant,

[Exit Philip R. Prince Julien L].

FOURTH SCENE.

Scene.—Exterior of the Palace f the Finance Minister, illuminated fr m
top to bottom. Enter Julien blowing horn vigorously. Palace windows are
thrown up and heads peep forth.

BARON VON DIETZ.—Watchman let's have a song,
chant us a merry ditty, come—a verse or two, and a
dollar shalt thou have for thy pains.

BARONESS VON DIETZ.—If it be original and telling, another dollar as recompense I'll add.

PRINCE JUL.— (Bowing low.) Gentl men and la-
dies, it shall certainly be a most telling one -a sort of an
epic—a poem, of which, I am proud to say, I'm author
of both song and music (Sings).

Ye who are sunk in the lurrows of care,
Waste not thy time in pulling thy hair;
But pray aye, pray, to the good St Francis.
To make ye lord of the nation's finances
Thou need'st never fear then a bankrupt's poor fate,
But dwell in good style, paid for by the State;
Robbing and stealing to thy heart's content,
Showing a foot-pad was thy natural bent,
Oh! how the people then shall groan,
Whilst ye pilfer their coffers to stuff thine own.

BARON V. D.—(Excitedly.) Insolent and intoler-
able puppy! dost thou affront me in my very strong-
hold? Dog. beast devil! But shou shalt pay bitterly
for this.

BARONESS V. D.—Thy saucy tongue needs charming. Who art thou, fellow?

PRINCE JUL.—(Bowing.) May it pleash thine lord-
ships un ladyships honors worships I vas only inten-
shoning to sing yous a nice pooty leeddle song. I be
Abraham Levi, the pirate of the money market, well
known to all of yous ladies un shentlemens

SIR ABRAHAM LEVI—(Angrily.) Holy Moses! hast
thou such a lying tongue? I swear I shall cut it out the
first time we're alone. I shall run thee through with
my trusty sword. Wretch, know that I am Abraham
Levi—Sir Abraham Levi, the banker!

BARONESS V. D.—Thou hast most foully offended
the house of Dietz. Think not that thou'lt escaped
unscathed, No, by St, Michael, no! (Turns, What, ho!
Castellan, what ho!

Baron Von Dietz, the Baroness, Sir Abraham, the guests, headed by the Castellan and two of his guardsmen, all rush pell-mell into the street. The Castellan fall down striking the pavement. Everybody, except the ladies, falls over him as they pass out of the house. Only the Baroness and a couple of ladies leave the house, and they, on beholding the confusion, scream and rush back, running to the window, look forth, everyone vociferates confusedly. Exit Prince Julien R, laughing, and blowing horn as flats close in.

FIFTH SCENE.

Scene.—Matilda's Cottage. Exterior view. Enter Prince Julien L.

PRINCE JUL.---Well, I'm inclined to think that the house of Dietz and Levi will hereafter have an aversion to watchmen, and the tuneful notes of the faithful guardians of the night henceforth to their ears most dismally discordant shalt sound.

Enter Rose from D in Cottage C.

ROSE.--Dear Philip, I knew by the clock that you must be about passing, so I stole away from the company to talk with thee a moment. Speak low. love, that none may weigh our language Art thou not happy? Tell me, darling, does it not give thee joy to see thy sweetheart?

PRINCe JUL.—(Aside.) It's evident that all this gushing affection is not intended for me. Yet, as I've taken the watchman's place, it would be absurd, in fact, out of character, not to love his girl--for such she must be--besides, I should be shirking a part of his,or rather, my duty. Scipio Africanus! but she's a beauty, a most bewitching charmer (Aloud.) Happy? pshaw! happy's no name for it. (Takes her hands.) Why,I'm way up in the twenty-seventh heaven. I'm now in the possession of the very beatification of bliss. Who could be otherwise than happy in the smiling sunshine of such an angel as thou art. Immortal powers! I thank thee for placing in my path so lovely a goddess.

ROSE.—Ah, I'm so glad thou dost so love me, dearest. It delights me to have thee acknowledge it so frankly. Oh, Philip, I do adore thee above everything I fear me, sometimes, the feeling that my heart contains for thee is almost a crime, 'tis so vast, so all-absorbing.

PRINCE JUL.—If it be a crime to love, 'twas a sin for which we are not answerable. But talk not so, the all-wise Ruler of the Universe ordained that man and woman should love each other. The great Omniscience himself is love. Oh, how beautiful it is to love.

Would that we might dwe l together to the end of the world, and then wing our way to some planet star and live forever in this union of souls.

ROSE. —My own sweet dear, thy tongue distil s a honey more precious than the hive contains, even as the perfumed flowers attract unto themselves the bee, so doth thine eloquence hold me   Oh, Philip, thou art the sunbeam that guilds the pathway of my existence.

PRINCE JUL. (Aside.) Philip certainly possesses a priceless jewel in this fair young innocence. She hath such a fascination about her that almost persuades me to change places with Philip, not only for a night, but for all time to come   In all my life I never beheld before so much beauty, loveliness and simplicity con,-bined in any human being, nor would I believed it possible if mine own eyes did not now observe it to be a tangible fact.

ROSE. (Breaking way.) I must leave thee, now, Philip, dear, lest they discover my absenee and won-der, good-by darling, until we meet again at "St Greg-ory's." I'll try not to keep thee waiting.

PRINCE JUL. (Seizing her.) "Heartsease," wouldst leave me thus, leave me so coldly, without one fond embrace, one parting kiss. No, no, my fairy, this can-not be, I must taste thy pretty rosy lips ere we can part.

ROSE. Philip I should certainly enter with zest into the spirit of thy desire were we not in the public street. You know that I would refuse thee nothing within the bounds of propriety. What if some strange passer-by beheld us? Surely, Philip, ye must have had a sly glass too much at the side door of some tav-ern to have grown so bold faced.

PRINCE JUL. "Faint heart never won fair lady." As for any one seeing us that's out of the question. Just let me show thee how easy it's done without any one being the wiser.

ROSE. No, Philip, no, thou dost forget that the angels' will see us. But—— but——

PRINCE JUL. But--- Why stop at but—? Ah, I have it. But is a conjunction, a conjunction relates to a union--a union of what? In this case it must mean a union of lips. Now as to the angels. No un-

easiness needst thou give thyself.   For they're good
fellows and wouldn't tell anybody.

Prince Julien now essays to kiss Rose.   She attempts to prevent him.   After a slight struggle he succeeds.

ROSE.   Philip, ye must behave better, (releases
herself), a bad boy art thou getting to be.

PRINCE JUL.   Why, my sweet precious, there's
nothing in the Ten Commandments against kissing,
and, furthermore, when ye wear two such ripe cherries
for lips, how canst thou blame me, who so love· the
fruit, for plucking it.

ROSE.   Philip, I know thou art not an habitual
drinker ; also allowance make I that this be New Year's
Eve, yet hearken to my words, and believe me when I
tell thee the wine cup 's a foe to be feared.   Though
he's apparently a very clever, bright-faced companion,
whose sparkling eyes e'en seem to say, ha, ha.   Yet in
his smile lurks destruction, and in his companionship
degradation and death, He is a tool to the devil.
The hangman's employer, and the curse to husband.
wife and children.   Oh, Philip I wish that our pecu-
niary circumstances admitted of our wedding sooner.
that I might watch o'er thee.

PRINCE JUL.   Not wed? nonsense, my darling
lass.   By the big boot of Milk Street, I'll marry thee
to-morrow.   Aye, cherub, to-night.   This very hour,
if thou'll consent.   Why I'll make it a regular business.
I'll--well, I will anyhow.   I'll——

ROSE.   I prithee stop; talk not such arrant foolishness.   Ah, love. I had a dream the other night.   Oh,
such a dream, it makes me sad to think of it.

PRINCE JUL.   (Taking her hands.) A dream.   Fie,
thou dost not. I hope, attach much significance to
dreams ?

ROSE.   No, but then—— Oh, pshaw. listen and
I'll tell it thee : I dreamed that thou hadst won a prize
in the lottery ; we were both so happy.   Thou hadst
purchased an elegant garden filled with such a diversi-
ty of beautiful flowers. and possessing a spacious hot-
house replete, with rare exotics and gay plumaged
songsters, whose notes rendered the place a second
Eden.   Such a fortune it would have been, Philip).
When I awoke suddenly, I felt so wretched and miserable. I wished I had not dreamed such a happy dream.
Thou hast nothing in the lottery, love, hast thou ?

(Looking wistfully). Have ye really won any hing, dearest ? The drawing took place to-day.

PRINCE JUL. How much must be the measure of my gain to pursuade thee into marrying me this very week ?

ROSE. A gain of eight or ten thousand dollars, would--goodness--but that's a great fortune. Say three or four thousand. This would buy a very pretty place in the suburbs, leaving unto thyself some goodly hundred beside.

PRINCE JUL. What if it were five thousand sweetheart ?

ROSE. Darling is it true ? Is it a bright reality ? Don't deceive me, it would be cruel. Worse than the wrack. Thou hast had a ticket and ye have won ; will they pay thee forthwith ? Tell me, Philip ?

PRINCE JUL. Yes, seraph, I've won. I now place my luck in thy hands (presents a purse) for safe keeping.

ROSE. (Accepting purse.) Philip, embrace me ; thou mayest kiss me, too, if thou like.

PRINCE JUL. (Mockingly.) Oh, but it's wrong to osculate in any place but the parlor, and there only when we're alone. Some one may observe us, and that would be dreadful. (Shaking finger.) I fear me thou hast taken too much New Year's Eve. Beware of the wine cup, 'tis a scurvy skunk, a very polecat to the breath. It will cause thee to perform antics that would make the devil grin, and the angels weep. It breedeth blear eyes and a red nose, ending in a case for young doctors.

ROSE. (Smilingly, while pocketing money). Thou art a saucy fellow to poke such fun at thy sweetheart. Yet, I'll forgive thee. There's no harm to kiss now, as the moon is under a cloud. It's only when she shines forth, Philip, and as for the angels--well, they'll rejoice at the happiness of two true loving souls.

PRINCE JUL. Thou art as ready with thy tongue as is my father's jester. I mean as is the Margrave's fool. (Aside.) By Lucifer I must be more guarded. (Aloud.) Thy budding charms are enough to make a hermit forget his vows. (Embrace and kiss) Precious thou'll make a most bewitching bride. (Aside.) Under all her guilessness I do observe an eagerness most pleasing. Playing watchman is quite to my taste, I think I'll act substitute for Philip very often. This girl will afford merry entertainment. (Aloud.) This then makes thee mine, (places a ring on one of Rose's fingers) my own (kisses her hand) my sweet one.

ROSE. No, not this petty bauble, this gewgaw, this bit of something, yet nothing. 'Tis the passion I bear thee that makes me thine. This bijou wears but the analogy of a witness to a bond. Why, man, if thou wast not my own dear, dear Philip, my darling lover, the wealth of Croesus could not possess thee of my heart's affection.

PRINCE JUL.—Not if I laid it at thy feet, a Princes' coronet to keep company with the riches of the Athenian whose name ye just spoke. And yet were not thine own dear, dear Philip.

ROSE.—No, I'd hurl the money and the coronet back to thee, for none but my Philip shall have me to wife; to clasp in fond embrace, to revel in the warmth and ardor of a bosom that's big with love. But I must hie away, dear, or they will mark my absence, good-bye, darling. [Both kiss at each other with hand.] Good-bye.

[Exit Rose C. into cottage.]

- PRINCE JUL [Shrugging shoulders.] Well, it's decidedly apparent that this girl is rather spooney on her Philip. Yet I think I'll have to study up her case, for the witch even excels my elfish cousin Louise, and such a possibility I once conceived could not evist. But this is hardly fair judgment. Louise is dark, whilst this bouquet of charms hath hair like the first blush of the morning sun. Poor cousin, she's a good, true woman, she imagines that I care but little for her; if she could only look into my heart she would not think so. After I've sown my wild oats I'll settle down with little Vesie. It's a pity this peasant girl is not one of the ladies of my Father's Court, then there would be some chance to win her over to my purpose. This, I must confess, is not saying much for Court Ladies, But suppose—pshaw, the idea of a peasant girl standing proof against the love of a Prince, non-sense. I'll have her as sure as fate. From what I've seen of women, it's my opinion that you're only to flatter them, and make them presents, and then—well, the rest is only a matter of time. This Cottage Queen

hath the handsomest face and the most enticing form
of any female that ever led me into mischief, I wonder what her name can be? Surely it must be a very,
very euphonious one. By all the gods, at once, she
shall be mine, even if I'm compelled to offer her mor-
ganatic marriage. Louise to this cannot object, and if
she does, why—well I'll have to exercise a little authority. Ah! footsteps, [Listens.] Coming this way,
(Steps to R.)

[Enter Paddy Yorick from L. I. E., and Professor Wisemann R. I. E.,
both in great haste, jostle each other with force, then stagger about and stare
at each other for a second.]

PADDY YORICK. (Seizing Prof. Wisemann's
hand.) Be heavens but its yer self. Ther top ov the
avenin' ter ye's. (Shakes Professor's hand vigorously.)
But its meself that's powerfully glad ter mate ye's. I'm
jist on the road ter yer house, sure, and it's mighty
happy I'll be when I git there, for it's outrageously
thirsty I am. Bedad, but its meself that knows who
kapes ther genuine stuff, the rael owld crature, and
whose not maine wid it ither. (Suddenly.) Begobs,
but what have ye in yer bag. Whare the divil are ye's
goin wid it?

PROFESSOR WISEMANN. (Making a wiy face.)
Pleased am I to meet thee Paddy. (Releasing his
hand.) But as I have occupation for my fingers I'm
of the opinion that they are safer out of thy reach.
(Examines hand.) "Shamrock," thou hast too much
feeling in thy friendship. Would'st know where I were
going? Well, I was going to the nocturnal meeting of
the "Fossil Cranium Club," to which ye know I am
the Professor of Fossilology. But as I have met thee,
I shall defer it to another meeting. As to what I have
in my bag, I'll answer thy interrogation by a question.
What hast thou in thine?

PADDY.—Ye's remember, I suppose, after I had
obtained the skulls of Sazer, Olexander and Tamber-
lain, ov promising me a goodly sum ov money if I procured for ye's the skull of Shakespoke, or Shakespeare,
as the thoroughbreds call 'em.

PROF. W.—Most clearly do I remember, but—

PADDY. (Waiving his shellalah.) Howld yer
whist man, it's not his but I'm after fetchin, its the
hid, yes sir, the skull ov Shakespeare. (Brings forth a
skull.) Behowled for yer self. Its just five or six

years now since the longwinded owld spalpean's been under the turf. I dug up his hid wid me own hands, so I did.

PROF. W.—This is impossible, Paddy. (Produces skull.) See, I already possess that great man's head It was—

PADDY.—An unprincipled rogue ov whom ye's bought it thin. A dirty vagabond to palm off such a fraud. 'Tis amazin the cheek that some folks have. Sure I wouldn't have belaved it ov anyone. Faiks, but havn't ye's an idea who it was.

PROF. W —Yes, he sold it to me about four or five weeks ago. I fear me it was thyself that was cheated, for it was none other than thy father.

PADDY. (Aside, looking confused and scratching his head.) Be heavens,but this takes the starch out ov me intirely. (Aloud,suddenly.) Begobs but I have it, ha-ha-ha, sure, en its as plain as me sherlalie. De yer mind ther small dimensions ov the skull in yer hand, remark ther narrer hocciput, ther undervelloped sinsyput, whare hintelligence is still mite. Forsooth, it's Shakespeare's, but Shakes as a kid, a kid about eight or tin years owld. Whareas, the wane thits in me own hand is Shakes as a man. What more proof do ye's want, now.

PROF. W.—Strange, yet forced am I to confess that thou art certainly correct in what ye say.

PADDY —Right, is it ? ov course I'm right, I niver was wrong but once in the hull ov me life, and thin I was right. Be the powers its the truth I'm after tellin ye's.

PROF. W.—Verrily, I'm in luck; two skulls of that mighty Builder of Plays, one when a boy and the other when a man. It seems as if Providence hath taken science under its especial care. Paddy, I'll crack an extra bottle of Green-seal to-night out of compliment to the manner in which thou hast labored in the cause of learning.

(They now both put back their respective skulls, each into its bag, drawing strings.)

PADDY.—Sure yer honor. I'd die for science.

PROF. W. [Taking Paddy's arm.] I know thou would'st, " Shamrock," I know thou would'st. Come.

PADDY.—Ter ther matein, is it, yer Honor?

PROF. W.—By no means. I'm too elated to dis-

cuss business ; even though that business relates to
Fossieology.   Come, it's to my dwelling we go.

PADDY.—I'm wid ye ivery time, yer honor.   Och,
bloody nouns, but its meself thit waz weaned upon
ther bottle, and ther bottle has stuck ter me iver since.
[Sings.]

> For it's I'm ther boy that's light of heart,
> And love ter drink good wine,
> Who belaves this life was set apart,
> For ter have a merry time.

(Exit Professor and Paddy, arm-in-arm, R. I. E.)

PRINCE JUL.   (Coming forward.)   Well, what
next.   (With emphasis.)   It hath always been a mystery to me, how Shakespeare, who possessed but a
limited education, wrote so wondrously fine, so gram-
matical, etc., etc., whilst I, with more than common
scholarship, find it quite a task to compose my own
pieces, either in prose or verse, in verse especially.
I'll admit that an ounce of genius is superior to a pound
of mere book learning ; yet to have written such a
work as did this British Bard, only through and by the
assistance of genius, was certainly marvelous.   But
alas, I have the whole secret discovered.   Solved the
problem   The mystery ceases to be a mystery.   For
who in thunder could'nt write, if they were a double-
headed cuss like this Dramatic inkslinger.   Ha-ha-ha,
Oh, what the world owes to learned Professors. to—
(Bell tolls the eleventh hour.)   Ah, Sir Watchman,
thou art forgetting thy duty·   Come, this will never
do.   (Blows horn.)   Toot-toot-tu, toot-toot-tu, toot-
toot-tu. (Calls.)   Eleven o'clock and all is well. (Sings.)
Ye are warned of the hour by the loud throated bell,
But its only the Watchman knoweth all is well.
[Horn.]   Toot-toot-tu, toot-toot-tu, toot-toot-tu.
Now for some more fun.   [Walks L.]   No, I'll naught
to do with this road.   [Comes R.]   I'll take this street.
Aye, this is the very route for me.

(Exit Prince Julien R.)

SIXTH SCENE.

SCENE.—A public square.   House on either side.   A statue of Ethelbert
C.   The river Rhine in the distance.   Enter Prince Julien L., followed by a
crowd of male citizens shouting.   Windows are thrown up and females look
out.   On reaching the statue the Prince gives a blast on horn, some of the
females come forth.

FIRST CITIZEN.   [To people.]   Make room good

comrades, our friend the Watchman be going to sing a
bit. (To Prince.) Come, my jolly lad, pipe us a verse.

(Enter Lieutenant Broadsword R, with a village girl leaning on his arm.)

SECOND CIT.—Now good Watchman do thy best.
Let it come from the heart lad, let it be with a will.

PRINCE JUL. (Singing.)
The traffic in our town is at a standstill,
    And sweet cupid disgusted, the place hath fled,
For our girls though they strive with eager good will,
    No beaux can they find, whose them willing to wed,
Though they pencil they eyebrows, and hang out their
        charms,
    And by their vain arts look really quite fair,
Yet still in the market, they stand with alarm,
    For no man it seems, wants such poor brittle ware.

LIEUTENANT BROADSWORD. (Pompously.) Fellow, darest thou to offer insult to the fair sex in the
presence of a soldier, an officer and a gentleman.

SECOND CIT.—Mr. Lieutenant, the Watchman
hath sung the truth, aye, the truth to the letter. That
jade by thy side is a most convincing proof of what I
say.

FIRST CIT.—Yea, yea, thou sayest correctly
neighbor. The devil fly away with all deceitful women
say I. (Throws down his hat and stamps upon it in a
rage.) If I had my way, I'd treat them after the
fashion of the Mahomedans.

VILLAGE GIRL. (Aloud.) St. Nicholas. (Aside
to Lieutenant as she hides her face.) That old man
is my betrothed husband. I thought he was off for a
month's stay. What shall I do? Oh, what shall I do?
I'll surely lose him. All his money will now go to
some institution. This is too bad; why did'nt the old
fool remain where he was.

FIRST CIT. (Shaking his finger at maid.) Aha,
thou art caught at last my saucy minx. It seems my
face is known to thee Why art thou so excited?
Aha, ye know full well. Is this the manner, is this the
way an affianced bride, aye a woman engaged to be
married should act? wandering and gadding about
town late at night with a stranger, a man totally unknown to thy betrothed husband. On the morrow thy
good father and mother shall hear of this; henceforth
I'll have nothing more to do with thee. From this
hour we are two.

THIRD CITIZEN.—My venerable friend I wouldn't give that brazen piece a moment's thought. The trull's not worth making a fuss about. Remember, there's as good fish in the sea as ere was caught. For a wife I wouldn't have yonder Jezabel, not if she was as rich as Solomon. I'll admit she hath face and form beautiful enough to tempt a man to sin, but not to marriage ; she's too bold. She's not a woman, she's a thing ; a thing to be at once despised and pitied—despised for her baseness, pitied that she hath not a will strong enough to resist evil, especially as she knows (and of the fact we are fully proven). that " As ye sow so will ye reap."

LIEUT. B. [drawing sword.]—I'll strike down to the very dust the first poltroon that dares say aught wrong of this fair creature. It doth amaze me, that any of ye have had the temerity to speak in the manner ye have in the presence of a soldier, an officer, and a gentleman.

SECOND CIT.—A right good time, my arrogant puppy, will ye have in fulfilling thy bragging words.

THIRD CIT.—Both of these citizens, Mr. Lieutenant, are to me well known, the girl beside thee, and that old man yonder ; I can vouch for the man being a worthy person, but as for that female, all that I've said I'll firmly adhere to, for know ye, sir, I never speak hastily, or without proof. Furthermore, I too endorse the Watchman's song. The reason of its truth is this . The women are getting stuffed up with ridiculous notions. They think of nothing but finery. Plain tradesmen refrain from entering into marriage, for fear the venture may swamp them. Who wants a giddy-headed wife, whose only thought is parties, balls, and dress. I believe in luxuries, and pleasant entertainments, if one can afford them, as much as anybody, but I don't think it shows a wise head to make a god of such things. Besides, a wife should have some time to give to her husband. They were bad enough, but ever since you soldiers have encamped in this quarter of our city they've gone crazy. It disgusts me to see what fools they make of themselves over the wearer of an epaulet, no matter whether under his gaudy uniform beats the heart of a cur or a villain; they're entirely given up to show· They can't seem to realize that ye " sons of Mars " are but toying with them. What's a soldier want with a wife, when he can get one in every town. Until this nonsense be done away with there'll be a large addition to the sisterhood of spinsters.

SECOND CIT.—I've little faith in women. I'm inclined to think that some of them are content with the groove in which affairs now run. In fact, I'm of the opinion that a goodly number of the spinsters of this town are married old maids.

Male citizens laugh ; female citizens rush into houses, and sally forth with brooms. The Lieutenant brandishes his sword, which is knocked out of his hand by the Staff of Prince Julien. The women beat the men with their brooms, everybody vociferates confesedly. The brooms are, after a struggle, taken from the women, who are chased into their houses. Some of the men sieze the Lieutenant, and divest him of his outer garments and trappings, others procure a large blanket, in which they place him and toss him high in the air. Prince Julien siezes the Village Maid by the waist, with one arm, and exits with her hurriedly. R.

SECOND ACT—FIRST SCENE·

SCEN .—Front view; high garden walls of a mansion ; a gate C gable and rear of the Palace boldly visible, surrounded with trees ; enter Philip. R.

PHILIP.—Have I done right in exchanging with this gay and frolicsome stranger, Pshaw ; have not I his word of honor, his promise, that no harm should befall my house, no matter what transpired. Surely he'll keep his honor unsullied, he will not insult his own word. He evidently is a gentleman, and a man of influence. Well, there's no withdrawing now. I think the best thing I can do ——

Enter Count Wortenburgh C. from garden gate, bows, then rushes up to Philip.

PHILIP [aside]. — What fantastic devil is this. [Aloud·] Stand out of my way fellow, I would pass on.

COUNT WORTENBURGH.- My gracious lord, in the deep meditation of thy royal mind thou hast noticed not the locality. and were about unintentionally to offer me an affront by passing my house this New Year's eve without entering. I did not know thou hadst returned from the wolf hunt in the Black Forest, or I would have sent Your Highness an invitation to the masked ball. But fie, my lord, there needs be no ceremony between us, for ye know full well ye are always an honored guest, come when ye will.

PHILIP—Wherefore Royal Highness me ; I am no gracious lord. Stand aside, sir, and let me pass.

COUNT W. [bowing]—Thy pardon, Prince. Yet if thou hast a desire to remain incognito your Excellence will remove that well-marked star, your High-ness; its a very telltale, a spy upon thyself.

(Philip takes off hat and attempts to remove star from it.)

COUNT W.—Stay, Lord Julien, I only spoke of the star to show thee that I know thee, for, assume whatever garb ye may, I'll recognize thee in it. Thou canst not disguise thyself from me; I'd know thee if only by thy noble presence. Yet if it were possible for me to have a doubt as to thy identity, the very attempt of thine to conceal the star upon thy hat would settle it. [Laughs.] You see, good Julien, there's no use of denying thyself to me.

PHILIP [aside, replacing his hat].—So, so; its the wild young Julien with whom I've exchanged. By St. Michael, he stated the truth when he said I'd nothing to fear. Ah, I grow bold. We shall now see who plays his part the best, Julien or Philip. From this time until I abdicate at "St. Gregorys," (unless I stumble o'er the Margrave), I am Crown Prince of Baden. (Aloud.) Sir, our Excellence awaits thy plea-sure, and admits all ye have said.

COUNT W.—Let us enter by the rear gate, here, as I came. Does your Highness intend to participate in the dancing?

PHILIP.—No. You see I have on my riling boots, and, therefore, have no place in this worthy trifling.

COUNT W.—Your noble Honor will play, then.

PHILIP.—No, neither can I partake of that sport. I have not sufficient money with me.

COUNT W.—By St. John. Why, my best of friends, does't thou suppose that Count Wortenburgh hast forgotten the many.services rendered him by Prince Julien? Here, my Lord, my royal brother, (puts a purse in Philip's pocket), accept this and pay me when ye like. Now thou art armed for the fray; come

(Count Wortenburg now leads Philip through garden gate C, and closes it after him.

SECOND SCENE.

SCENE.—Interior of Wortenburg Palace. A grand saloon, brilliantly lighted and superbly furnished, a harpsichord L. C., table, R. C. Music heard as if coming from the Ball Room. Sultan, Sultanesses, Gypsies, Knights in armor, nuns, goddessess satyrs, monks, Medes, Persians, Chaldeans, Sprites, Peries, Fairies, Soldiers, and ladies and gentlemen in Court costume all masked. The assemblage flits in couples, etc., in Conservatory, which is arched and situated at the rear of saloon, appearing now and then to en-, ter and leave Ball Room. All discovered.

(Enter Count Wortenburgh and Philip. R.)

COUNT W.—Sir Prince, wilt thou go to the hazard table, or wilt thou first—

PHILIP.—My Lord Count, let's first drink to the success of the masquerade ; then sir I'm thine to command.

COUNT W.—With all my heart, dear Julien, with all my heart (Pulls bell cord.) God knows, I wish it successful, more ways than one.

[Enter Servant R.]

SERVANT. (Bowing,) Thy pleasure, gentlemen.

COUNT W.—Bid the caterer prepare (if he has it not ready) a decanter of mulled wine, and bring it here thyself immediately.

SERVT.—Excuse me gentlemen, but if ye prefer, I'll to the banquet hall conduct ye both.

COUNT W.—Go to, confound it man, I didn't call thee to consult with thee. Art thou the Grand Factotum of this house. If ye please, I'll direct things to my liking, not thine. Do as I have commanded thee, and let not grass grow under thy feet.

(Exit Servant R., bowing.)

PHILIP.—Count, when e're it may please thee to engage in the joyous dance, let not my society at all hinder thee.

(Enter Servant R. with decanter and two wine glasses, on a salver; sets wine down on table R. C., bows and exits. Philip and the Count now each fill a glass.

COUNT W. (Holding out his glass.) Here's to the success of the masquerade.

PHILIP. (Striking the Count's glass with his.) Aye, to the success of the masquerade, a happy ending of the old year, and a bright beginning of the new.

(Philip and the Count now each drain their glasses.)

COUNT W. My good Lord Julien, I, like thyself, shall refrain from dancing. No pleasure now doth this fine sport vouchsafe unto me, even sweet music (an art in which ye know I am no Tyro) ; music in which I once did revel, hath no more the power to stir my soul. Oh, Julien, Julien, my best of friends, surely thou must be acquainted with the why of " Terpsicho-

re's lost power to charm me. I have so far deceived
my acquaintances into believing me happy and content. I gave this ball with sworn intentions to convince
those who may doubt. But, oh, what a savage jest.
To be sure I drink and play at cards more than ever,
but though I seem to be satisfied with the turn of
affairs, I lie—and the lie is choaking me. I am one
moment gloomy and taciturn, and the next careless
and flippant. As a chameleon doth change its color,
so I change my moods. Oh, bear with my shiftings of
spirit, for my heart is heavy and joy hath fled me.

PHILIP. The language of Nobleman Wortenburgh, to me is an enigma, I am not apt in guessing,
my good Lord Count.

COUNT W. Is it possible, Sir Prince, that thou
dost not know of my troubles? Dost not know that
the Princess De Albeaux of France, she whom I idol-
ized, and who I thought sincerely loved me in return,
hath broken with me; aye, most cruelly and suddenly?

PHILIP. I must confess, gentle Sir, that what
thou hath just now spoken is to me quite cloudy—in
fact 'tis a mystery.

COUNT W. Say ye so; knowest thou naught
whatever of what happened me at Mount Blanc?

PHILIP. Nothing, my good Lord, nothing. Not
even so much as an iota of one poor hint.

COUNT W. Then list, your Highness. You remember that the Queen of Spain paid a visit to the
Margrave (your father), last summer—somewhere in
August—and that the Margrave (her cousin,proposed a
trip to Mount Blanc, which proposition was accepted
and carried into effect? That, along with the rest, the
Princess and myself were invited, as was also the Baroness of Walderstein. I was unable to go with the
party, yet, as they travelled the distance in no hurry,
I was enabled to overtake them just as they were about
to do the mountain. I did not observe the Princess—
in fact I dreamed not that she was along, she having
told me she could not go. The Queen and the Baroness were the first to greet me. Thy Royal relative
(the Queen) instantly appointed me Cavalier to the
Baroness. Not being aware of my preference for the
Princess, just as we were about to start, I discovered
my beloved Charlotte; yet, what could I do but pro-

ceed. Which I did, leaving the Princess under the care of their Most Sovereign Excellencies,the Margrave and the Queen. For this Charlotte bears me hard. It is the cause of her breaking with me, for she hates the Baroness, and looks upon her as a rival. She hath returned my picture and all my letters, demanding a reciprocity of action. She will not believe that, though with the Baroness, my heart was with her. Oh, would that I had absent been, when my lady, the Queen, stepped foot in this fair city.

PHILIP. Thy case is a sad one, Sir Count, thou art much to be pitied. Yet, if thou art wise, thou wilt take advantage of the present joyous season, and strive anew to prevent the budding of New Year's Day on thy severed friendship. Do this and thy masquerade will surely be a success, and our toast not drank in vain.

ENTER—Princess De Albeaux C, from the Conservatory: unobserved and unobserving. Takes off mask on striking saloon. Crosses to Harpsichord L. C, and seats herself, pretends to be fixing mask as she enters and until addressed by Philip.

COUNT W. I shall endeavor to do so, for she is here ; but thinks I know it not. She comes to watch, imagining she may discover something between the Baroness and myself. She intends (so I have ascertained by the merest chance) to leave before the time for unmasking, so that I shall not be aware of her having been here. (Suddenly beholding Princess.) Ave Maria. but here she is—aye, in the very room with us. Look yonder, by the Harpsichord, she does not see us. She thinks she is alone.

Philip looks, then crosses to Harpsichord. Princess starts as he approaches. Then arises and fixes her eyes steadily upon him.

PHILIP. Be not disturbed, for I come as a friend. Neither be ye angered with thyself cause thou art discovered, for thy lover and I knew that ye wert here, ere thou didst enter this saloon. Didst thou imagine that the loveliness of Princess Charlotte could be once beheld and e'er forgotten ? That a simple mask could disguise such grace ? Oh, no, thou hast deceived thyself, sweet lady, (bows). Madam, I came not to flatter, but to serve thee.

PRINCESS DE ALBEAUX, (Sternly·) Prince Julien (for I know thou art he), a few days ago thou wert entirely too bold. 'Tis unworthy of a man to spend his time as thou dost. I pray you, if thou dost value thy peace, never to attempt to make so familiar with me again.

PHILIP. (Bowing.) Etherious and bewitching lady, if Julien hath offended thee, I am sorry. See, thou canst trust me, I am quiet—quiet as an innocent lamb—aye, more quiet than ever ye saw Julien.

PRINCESS DE A. For that I'm thankful, as I shall not have to keep guard 'gainst thy attacks, Sir Prince.

PHILIP. Take no offence, your Highness, at the question I'm going to propound : Hast thou encircled thy sweet form in this Carmelite mantle to do penance for thy sins ; tell me, fair lady ?

PRINCESS DE A. (Haughtily.) Sir, this can be no business of thine ; furthermore, I've nothing to make atonement for. It is not well for people to be overwise.

PHILIP. What, Madam, thy harsh and unfeeling treatment of that sorrowing " Brahmin " yonder, ye needs do penance for ; 'tis cruel injustice.

PRINCESS DE A. I understand thee not, my lord.

PHILIP. To make my meaning plain, then, my lady, permit me to inform thee that this Brahmin is none other than Count Wortenburgh, the Chamberlain. He is as innocent as is thyself in the affair of Mount Blanc. He swears upon his soul 'tis true. Thou hast been too hasty, my lady.

PRINCESS DE A. (Looking surprised.) Why didst thou not inform me long ere this, oh, cruel, cruel, Julien ? What was thy reason for acting in such a fashion ? Ah, I see, ye thought, through spite, to work thine amorous plottings on me, me a lady. Sir, thou hast yet to learn how a true woman prizes virtue. My Lord, thou dost much displease thy noble Father in the color of thy actions.

PHILIP. I fear me that ye speak the truth about Prince Julien. Ethelbert is too good a father. But, come, the poor Count will die if thou dost not take him back to love. See, even under his mask, how easily thou canst discern agony working on his brow, and sadness sitting enthroned upon his heart strings.

PRINCESS DE A. Your grace is an eloquent intercessor. (with emphasis.) Ye plead Count Wortenburgh's cause almost as warmly as thou didst argue (some thirty days ago) for thine own vile purpose,

with my lovely little maid, Henrietta. Thank Heaven
I overheard thee, for now the child issafe, Julien, dost
thou ever think of what a man thou art becoming?

PHILIP. A truce, fair lady ; let bygones be bygones. Let's, like the Indians of that far distant
land—America, "bury the hatchet."

PRINCESS DE A. Julien, here (extending her right
hand) is my hand. I'll be friends with thee so long as
thou art with me. But as for the count, I'll forgive—
or rather renew our engagement, on one condition, and
that is that he resigns the office of Chamberlain ; it
brings him too much into the society of Court Ladies
for my liking. That Baroness—

PHILIP. The issue now at stake must be arranged
and settled on by Lord Wortenburgh and Lady De
Albeaux.

*Philip now leads the Princess to the Count, and places her hand in his;
Count and Princess embrace.*

COUNT W. My Charlotte, my own sweet Charlotte, my darling once again. (To Philip.) Sir, thou
hast made me supremely happy. (Grasps Philip's
hand.) Julien, henceforth thou can'st not count on a
truer friend than Wortenburgh. May ye live to be as
honored as thy father. I'd die for thee, Julien.

PHILIP. Stay, Sir Count, die not yet, the lovely
Charlotte hath use for thee, thou dost owe her a honeymoon. I prithee live at least till that's fulfilled.

COUNT W.   ⎞   ⎧ My Lord.
PRINCESS DE A. ⎭ Together. ⎨ Your Highness.

PHILIP. (Waiving his hand authoratatively.) Get
thee gone, and on pain of receiving my displeasure,
speak not to me again until Hymen hath made ye
'twain as one flesh.

*Exit Count and Princess C. into Conservatory. Princess remasking be-
fore making exit. They both throw kisses to Philip before leaving.*

PHILIP. I wonder how Julien will relish the dex-
terous manner in which I've manipulated and man-
ouvered in this case of heart's disease.

Enter in great haste L. General De Baldwin.

GENERAL DE BALDWIN. My Lord, where is the
Rose girl ?

PHILIP. [Aloud.] Selling her flowers, I suppose
[Aside.] Another Court mystery, I'll wager. [Aloud.]
Wherefore ask me ? What is a Rose-girl to me, sir,

I'd like to know? Man, thou dost most strangely talk.

GENL. DE B. Your grace, she is everything to me, sir; she is my wife. My Lord, I'm nearly crazed. If thou would'st prolong thy days, think no more of her; aye, sir, think no more of her.

PHILIP. Surely, I can think no less about her than I do; as I never thought of her seriously in my whole life. This, sir, I'm willing to swear to as a fact.

GEN DE B. Your Highness, I am resolved, my course is set; 'twill be useless to attempt to deceive me any more. I have sworn to kill thee if ye pay court to my wife any more; when my back is turned or at any other time. I shall find thee out, and I shall be sure to keep my word; I care not for the consequences.

PHILIP. Who art thou that talks in this fashion?

GEN. DE B. I have the honor to be General de Baldwin, a native and a Field Marshal of Saxony. I am Count of Leipsic. son of his Highness, the Duke of Chemnitz. You, Sir, are Julien, Crown Prinee of Baden. Attempt not to deny it. for it is useless. (Producing a paper.) Behold this 'tis, a missive my false wife intended for thee. (Holds it in front of Philip's face.) Read, Sir, read.

PHILIP. (Aloud.) Dear Julien, be on thy guard, my husband hath suspicion that we have been carnally intimate. The Dutchess of Trent gives him to understand that she hath proof of all that transpired at the ball, which you remember took place at Sir Eric Wiertz's Castle. If I only had the envious wench by the hair for about five minutes I'm of the opinion she'd repent of meddling with what concerns her not. Yours in haste, Juno.

By St. Stephen, I swear that this was certainly never intended for me. I don't burden my thoughts or trouble myself in the least about thy wife, or the wife of any other man. My Lord General. I'm above such villainy. Jealousy hath surely obscured thy perspicacity. If thou didst but know me, with such baseness ne'er wouldst thou couple me. Again I swear to thee that I never have, nor ever shall I trouble thy wife.

GEN. DE B. Art thou in earnest? Can it be possible that ye speak the truth?

PHILIP. Most assuredly I'm in earnest, but remember there are more Juliens than one—at least I'm not the person for whom this note was written. Besides the "Juno" who hath signed her name to this epistle may not, after all, be thy wife.

GEN. DE B.   But, Sir, I am too well acquainted with her style of hand-writing to be deceived in regards to the note. I am confident she wrote it, but whether it was intended for thyself, or some other person, I'm now not so satisfied.

PHILIP.   Well, since thou art so determined to have it that she hath sinned, I will speak candidly, I did wish to shield thy wife from a discovery. The which cannot add to thy happiness. I trusted that the diffir culties that she hath had to pass through to keep her sin a secret to thee, might prove a lesson—a lesson so severe that she would never repeat her crime. I have strongly differed with thee. But now I do inform thee I believe she did commit the act of which thou dost accuse her, but by all the Gods at once, I swear 'twas not with me. 'Tis the fashion of too many wives to love somebody in the absence of their husbands. But, though it be true, yet am I loth to so acknowledge 'tis a high-toned thoroughbred, courtly fashion. That ye, like the general run of fast husbands, set up for thyself, and, as a true man, resent it most scornfully when it comes home unto thee. Dost think, my Lord, that the male portion of mankind alone have a privilege to carnal indulgences? In fact have as it were a patent right to be lascivious and immoral. If thou dost so conceive, thou art most woefully astray; sin is sin, and takes its color not from sex. Sir, for the last time, I swear I've had nothing to do with thy wife.

GEN. DE B.   Prince Julien is bitter to-night, Sir; I will believe thee what thou hast said—that is, I will believe to be sincere if thou wilt assist me in getting her to leave this place immediately. Persuade her to visit her relatives in France. Anything, I care not what, so long as she leaves this state. For once out of it, I wager my head she ne'er will enter it again. Do this and I will bless thee. Seek her out forthwith, your Grace, and do it to-night. Ah, I came near forgetting it. she has (from what I've discovered of her evening's plan) about changed her disguise—appearing now as a Spanish widow.

PHILIP.   My Lord General, I shall do my best to serve your Highness.

GEN. DE B.   Thanks, Prince Julien, I leave it entirely in thy hands (Bows.) Adieu for the present .

Exit General De Baldwin C, into Conservary.   Returns in haste, and rushes off L.

PHILIP.   Well, I'm certainly doing a thriving business in settling family jungles. Talking is dry work, I'll take a little more wine. (Fills and drains glass.) This will loosen my tongue and give me the courage requisite to go through with my undertaking,for it bids fair I'm to have my hands full.

Enter Lady de Baldwin C, from Conservatory, approaches Philip stealthily. Then peers into his face.

LADY DE BALDWIN.   Ah, Lord Julien, you here, really I'm glad—in fact I'm delighted—fortune is with me to-night.

PHILIP.   (Aside.) 'Tis the General's wife, as I live. (Aloud) Ye say fortune is with thee to-night. That is not strange, fortune ought to travel in the company of lovely women. Thou art happy. Well, that's as it should be, Beautiful widows find no lack of comforters. Most men think it a bewitching occupation -- that of consoling and solacing handsome widows Why hath the flowers of the rose girl withered so soon ?

LADY DE B.   What is there my Lord, that does not wither ? Is it the constancy of man's love for woman ? While passing through the Conservatory with Captain Vosburgh a short time ago, I saw thee deeply engaged in conversation with a certain Carmelite, and whom I knew to be (from the fact that she was unmasked) the Princess De Albeau; Julien ye are not false. but ye are fickle--fickle as the wind that blows.

PHILIP.   Accuse and berate me if ye will, yet I think I can return the accusation, freighted with more truth,

LADY DE B.   Will your Lordship be so good as to inform me in what respect ?

PHILIP.   Why, for example, we'll take thy worthy spouse. He loves thee and is proud of thee—admitting him somewhat too fast. Yet a good husband hath he been to thee. Thou shouldst love him tenderly, and with more fidelity. A true mother would not tarnish her children's birth, her offsprings' honor.

LADY DE B.   Prince, thou dost speak truly—a grievous wrong have I committed in listening to thy advances and yielding to thy embraces. I did at first repent, and even now, though wearing evil intent in my heart, I am sorry—sorry that I've got in such a tangle. But the thing is done, remorse, therefore comes too late.

PHILIP. No, never too late. Lets repair the mischief. Lets pour oil on the troubled waters. We'll bury the past, and henceforth our actions towards one-another shall be guided by the Ten Commandments. What say you, my sister, art thou with me ?

LADY DE B. Aye, with all my heart, good brother. Julien, I wish thy noble father could hear thee now, it would so please him to see his son rise above the libertine and tempter. My lord, 'tis true I have committed a base act, as has thyself. But ye shall not outdo me in making atonement. Right glad will I be when this stain upon my escutcheon is hidden in the night of time. Gay have I appeared, but my happiness was not real, 'twas not solid. A kind of pleasure may be extracted from sinfulness, but those who strive for it will most certainly be taught 'tis not worth the price which they'll be forced to pay. Surely will the cankerworm of conscience gnaw, and make his gnawings most tangibly felt. Julien, why didst thou not take on this mood some nights ago, then, perhaps, I ne'er had sinned. God forgive me, for though I've erred, yet do I love my husband. Oh, that the past were again the future, that my husband had never left my side. Would that I'd never seen a Court, or laid mine eyes upon thee. Then no insidious tongue could have misled me. Then I should never have fallen a victim to glut the sinful appetite of Prince Julien.

PHILIP. Hold, madam, hold, I too cry out " Peccavi, Peccavi.'* Yet 'tis written that those who see their error, acknowledge it, and strive sincerely to repent, are not hopelessly lost to proper life, nor all depravity. I believe with a certain poet, that though innocence may fall, and lose her white robe, yet by repentance may she again become possessed of the self-same garment. Mark me, thy husband has returned ; he is possessed in some manner of a knowledge of our intimacy ; that is, I should say, he hath a misgiving that things are not as they should be. I stung him somewhat severely, yet I'll wager the stinging will set

* L. I have sinned, I have sinned.

him thinking, and redound to thy benefit. Furthermore, I was successful in removing the suspicion from —from myself. You see its better he should think it anybody than Ethelbert's son. Yet, with a little tact we, or rather you (for it rests with thyself, now,) may convince him, that he hath fallen into error, for love, though not exactly blind, is a trifle near-sighted. Go to him and be true. The fidelity of a wife, a mother, is the pride of a family, of greater value than the emblazonry carved upon their shields.

Exit Lady De Baldwin L, as her husband enters R.

GEN. DE B. Dear Julien, I saw my wife enter here from the conservatory as I left thee, a few minutes ago. I saw her coming just as I had entered the conservatory myself. That's the reason I returned so hastily and fled by this door, (points to the door through which he had made exit). I watched without until I saw her leave, and now I'm here to know the issue. Is all well—tell me.

PHILIP. 'Tis more than well—'tis most excellent, the manner in which things have shaped themselves. Friend, thy wife may have erred—and she may not have erred. To speak frankly, judging from all I've recently heard, I'm inclined to give her the benefit of a doubt. I feel it is but fair.

GEN. DE B. Thou hast a big heart after all, Julien, my friend, and I am greatly indebted to thee for the service which thou hast rendered me this night. Oh, by the way, I came near forgetting a prior debt (hands a paper). Accept this order on my banker. 'Tis the sum I lost at cards to you some little time ago. E'er this thou should have had it, if I had met thee sooner. I leave thee now for my wife, and may Heaven bless thee.

Shakes Philip warmly by the hand. Exits C, through Conservatory.

PHILIP [Inspecting paper]. Well, my royal General, I'm very glad thou hast remembered to pay thine honest debt An order on thy banker for five thousand dollars is not bad to take, especially as this is New Year's Eve. This certainly is what might be termed a regular windfall. I begin to dread the hour when I must return my Coronet and vacate my throne.

Enter Colonel Bloomingdale, R hastily.

COL. BLOOMINGDALE. Julien, Julien, my lord,

we are both discovered. I shall lash me to one of my cannon and blow myself to atoms.

PHILIP [aside]. Another noble courtier in the meshes of a closely woven trouble. [Aloud.] What wouldst thou with me? Who art thou?

COL. B. I am Col. Bloomingdale. Her worship Theodosia, Mayoress of Carlsruhe, hath this night, aye, ten minutes ago, told Gen. De Baldwin's father about the joke we played on him a few evenings ago. Prince Herman is as mad as a white elephant. He swears—

PHILIP. And he is welcome to swear—to the end of the masquerade, for aught care I. What says your Honor?

COL. B. That there's no use of attempting to make light of the affair. It's the worst scrape (or, rather, I fear will turn out the worst) that ever we had to do with. He declares he'll press us hard for making him appear so ridiculous as we did at Epstein's. This very night I may be arrested and taken to the fortress jail, for he hath sworn to inform the Margrave. No, that shall never come to pass. I'll take my life first.

PHILIP. Stay, comrade, there's no need of that. Ethelbert cannot be yet acquainted with this secret, for thou hast just said Prince Herman hath sworn to inform the Margrave. Hath sworn is an act (we may say) wanting performance to give it shape. The act, therefore, (to my mind) is yet in the future tense. It has yet to germinate into the preterit before thou canst consider with strict certitude thou art in real danger. But how comes it the Mayoress is possessed of all these facts.

COL. B. 'Tis that what bothers me. Confound the witch, I shall be disgraced—I'm lost, lost to my profession, if ever your father becomes cognizant of this affair, Julien. I don't blame the Duke of Chemnitz for being incensed, for his back must yet be sore, and well marked and corrugated, as I bestowed upon him no gentle cudgelling. I'm lost, and so is the confectioner's daughter. I'll throw me into the Rhine at once.

PHILIP. Let not thy mind take much of grief on account of the confectioner's daughter, she, like thyself, will come from this difficulty with flying colors. Thou art entirely too tragicomic, my dear boy.

COL. B. Sir Prince, I prithee not to mock at my despair. I tell thee plainly I see no sense in the levity of thy last remark.

PHILIP. Be more cool and collect my noble Colonel. Don't froth and foam so. Thou wouldst lead any one (by cutting up in this fashion) to imagine that ye had the hydrophobia.

COL. B. Prince Julien, I'm astonished—I cannot comprehend how thou canst be so damned apathetic—so indifferent as to what I've told thee. If the dutchman who performed the part of Necromancer was only here he might extract us from our present difficulty, for he had a quick wit backed by a ready tongue. As it is he's escaped all the troubled of the scrape. I wish I were as safe as is that Hollander.

PHILIP. So much the better for us that he's not to be found, for since he hath hidden himself so securely, and as he dare not show his face, nor contradict that which we may say, we can, in the easiest possible manner, make a sort of scapegoat of him—in fact, throw all the blame upon his shoulders.

COL. B. Ah, that would be all very well if we could so arrange it, but it will not work, even though the cursed necromancer dare not reveal himself. Listen, the Mayoress dislikes both you and I, and, becoming possessed of our secret (for the present, it matters not how), has, on the first opportunity (which opportunity was this very night) told everything to the Duke, so of course his Highness has the whole catalogue, which reads thus.

"Prince Julien, being desirous to break off a match that had been agreed upon between Prince Herman—Duke of Chemnitz and his lovely Aunt, the Princess Maria; and being informed that Prince Herman was a very superstitious man, devised a scheme to procure from him something by which he could prevent marriage ever taking place between said parties. That in all these plottings he (Julien) was assisted by his bosom friend, Col. Bloomingdale. That they inveigled him into this trap and procured the consummation of it, exactly to the spirit of Prince Julien's desire. That is, obtained certain damning evidence—which you (Julien) now hold against him. That not only Prince Julien and Colonel Bloomingdale were into the plot. But also Captain Hoffman's niece and the confectioner's daughter; that a certain conjurer was procured at a very considerable cost to manage the trick. That the said Professor Schneider (such being his name and title), instructed the confectioner's daughter (who acted the spirit, and with whom he was infatuated), how to ensnare him. That I was the person who knocked him down, cudgelled and belabored him 'til he bellowed and yelled like a wild bull. If I had only not carried the joke too far, but I was desirous of cooling his passion a little for my sweetheart. 'Twas a miserable—an infernal business. By St. Paul but I'll throw me upon my sword.''

PHILIP. Tut, man, throw thyself into the arm's of thy lady, 'tis much more pleasant; besides let me inform thee its not in keeping with thy noble calling and exalted title to talk so of taking thy life—fie, and that too four or five different ways—simply because thou hast met with a difficulty in which ye fear ye may suffer a trifle, or, a little more than relishable. If you act after this fashion a real soldier you never would become.

COL. B. Julien, if thou art my friend make not of me, I prithee, a target for thy merriment. By all the furies, but this is the most complex affair I ever had the bad luck to become entangled with. Your Highness, I hope ye have the paper safe wherein the Duke did sign to take the confectioner's daughter to his house and keep her as his mistress, after he had married with thy relative, etc.

PHILIP. 'Tis safe. (Aside.) A most entertaining narrative, this (aloud.) Why, behavior of this color would be even a disgrace amongst the commonest people. The meanest and lowest citizens who calls good Ethelbert Sovereign, could scarcely conduct themselves in a worse fashion.

COL. B. Indeed, my Lord, your Highness speaks the truth. 'Tis impossible to behave more meanly and vulgarly than the Mayoress, for we have both always treated her with the utmost politeness. As for myself, I could swear I never gave her any cause to take such a dislike as she seems to hold against me.

PHILIP. Then, most noble Colonel, dost thou forsooth forget thyself? Thou hast given her cause, and so has Prince Julien. Are not Julien and Bloomingdale a couple of reprobates? And is that not sufficient to cause for themselves, the contemptand dislike of so exemplary a lady as her Honor, the Mayoress.

COL. B. Well, Prince, be that as it may, ye must interpose thine influence with thy Royal father in my behalf. Come, thou shalt not leave me until ye promise.

PHILIP.—Where is the Duke, Sir Colonel, hast thou any idea ?

COL. B. I left Miss Hoffman's mother on his track. She will endeavor to keep him from the Margrave until we have hit upon a plan of defense. We've no time to lose, Julien, Prince Herman, said the Margrave, should hear of this business ; should be notified of the manner visitors are treated while enjoying the hospitality of his court, and I tell thee. sir, the old man means to keep his word, yet I think he can be quieted by the document in your possession. I——

PHILIP.—Yes, yes, man, o'erleap all incident, answer me. Where is Prince Herman ?

COL. B. I suppose he's endeavoring to gain (quietly) the ear of the Margrave.

PHILIP. Great Cæsar, and is the Margrave really here ?

COL. B. Yes, he unexpectedly dropped in--I say unexpectedly, because he gave out he would not be here ; a fact I suppose thou art better aware of than myself. He arrived just before I came here--he's not in mask. From what I saw before I lett, I presume he's now about engaging with the Minister of Police in a game of cards. As your Grace is so good at scheming I'll leave everything to thee, my thoughts are too mixed to be of any assistance ; I'll see thee at about two A. M., as we might be watched. It will not do for us to be found together at present ; I hope we'll navigate safely through the " Charybdis " of this business. I must leave thee now [Bows.] Adieu my Royal friend

(Exit Col. Bloomingdale C, through Conservatory, hastily.)

PHILIP. So so, a couple of merry lads are they— this Julien and his friend. By St. Luke—if our good Ethelbert hears of this, it will be hard to tell who'll be wrecked on " Scylla " first, the Civic or the Military Prince. For the Margrave will not favor evil doing any more in his son than any other citizen. By jove its high time I were again that high functionary, the

" Cerberus " of the night. I fear me I'm getting myself and my substitute into a position we'll find too dif-
ficult from which to extract ourselves. What vulgar
things are done in. Palaces. What vile actions are
committed by the rich—with impunity. They to whom
the poor are taught to look for refinement and moral
instruction ; they who are termed the upper class —the
better. By my troth but as actions speak louder than
words, I should say that they were the lowest class, if
I'm to consider those with whom I've just been associa-
ting—people of quality, well—

(Enter Baron Stamwitz R.)

BARON STAMWITZ. [In subdued voice—laying
hand on Philip's shoulder.] All alone my Lord. That's
good, for I have something private to say to thee,
something that will benefit both of us. May I have
the pleasure of your Highness's attention for a moment,
the business is of a most urgent nature.

(Philip removes the Baron's hand, then steps back a pace.)

BARON S. Oh it's all right my Lord—I'm Baron
Stamwitz,cousin of Baron von Dietz,the Minister of Finance, I am the State's Treasurer, I hope your Grace
enjoyed the Wolf hunt.

PHILIP. Well my Lord Treasurer ; what commands hast thou.

BARON S. I shall speak openly and to the point,
Sir Prince ; I was about broaching this matter to thee
before thy hunting expedition took place, but I thought
I had better await thy return, imagining it would please
thee more, and that thou vouldst in thy leisure be
better able to contribute thy Royal assistance. Your
Highness must be aware, that there's no one in all the
broad lands that compose this "Margraveate" who
take more pleasure in serving thee, than the Finance
Minister, and his colleague the Treasurer of Baden.

PHILIP. If thy words emanate sincerely from thy
heart, then I say Julien is most truly grateful. But my
mind falls shrewdly to the belief, that there's no de-
pendence to be placed on the honeyed words of smooth
tongued Courtiers. Make known thy business my Lord.
with as much brevity as possible.

BARON S. Well, your Highness is pleased to be
severe, nevertheless—be it known to your Grace, the

House of Sir Abrahan Levi has applied to us (the Finance Minister and myself), about the fifty thousand dollars he advanced your Royal Highness. He says he must have the money immediately, or he will apply to the Margrave.

PHILIP. Will he keep his threat—can't you my Lord, induce the old man to wait.

BARON S. He will Sir Prince; he will wait about as much as will the Goldsmith Brothers, who demand that their seventy-five thousand dollars shall be put into their hands without another moments delay.

PHILIP. Well, I suppose if the people will not wait for their money, why I must—

BARON S. Stay your Highness—be not rash, the Minister and I are in a position to relieve—in fact to make everything comfortable, if—if—

PHILIP. If what, my Lord Baron

BARON S. If thou wilt agree to the following, you see Sir Abraham Levi has bought up immense quantities of grain; a decree against importation, will increase the price considerably. By obtaining for Levi the control of the market, thou wilt be the gainer, thus: He agreeing to pay for the monopoly, fifty thousand dollars down. To erase thy former debt of the same amount, and liquidate the seventy-five thousand dollars owing to the Goldsmith Brothers, but everything depends npon the present Finance Minister and Treasurer remaining at the head of the Fiscal Departmet. If Dr. Steinberg succeeds in ejecting us from office, we are incapacitated from rendering unto your Highness the service mentioned. Now all that we ask my Lord, is that thou wilt use thine influence with thy noble father and have us retained in our present dignities. We don't seek the position for the position's sake, or because we think there's plenty of money to be made, but only to serve your Grace; for to be candid, Baron Von Dietz and myself are tired of office, and if it were not that we held your Excellence's comfort and pleasure above our ease, we would straightway proceed to take rest by tendering our resignation.

PHILIP If I comprehend thee aright Sir Treasurer, thou wouldst starve the poor a little (I say the poor, for upon them would the burden really fall), in order to rid me of my debts; consider, my Lord, the sufferings thou wouldst produce. Surely it would never do to let this come to the ears of Ethelbert.

BARON S. We do not propose that it shall come to the ears of the Margrave, we are of the opinion of your Highness most emphatically, as to its being dangerous, yet in the face of all risks and hazards I here state we will take all such burdens on our shoulders, in fact my Lord, we guarantee to stand for everything, of course————

PHILIP. One moment, please. I cannot see how the Margrave's to be inveigled into issuing a decree against the importation of grain.

BARON S. We will manage that quite cleverly— aye, by the very love he bears for the people, his country. By this, his old hobby. 'Tis the duty of a Ruler to protect the industries of the state over which he presides. You see we will make it appear to him that our trade in grain is being seriously interfered with by unscrupulous foreign dealers, who are enabled to undersell our countrymen, because they furnish to the millers a worthless article at a reduced value. We will request executive interposition on behalf of the grain raising interest of our land. We will shower him with forged petitions from our citizens, of course we are aware that after we have seduced the Margrave into signing the decree (which we shall take special care to draft with our own pen and ink), he will in the course of a month (sooner or later) perceive that he has made a mistake. (For to speak the truth, my Lord, judging from our reports, grain of our own raising is more scarce than plenty.) Has miscalculated, as it were, that instead of an abunndance there is u dearth. That we must look elsewhere than to our planters for breadstuff.

PHILIP. Well, what then—of course we're all discovered.

BARON S. Not so, my lord. We will inform him that all was right at first. But, that a strange bug got into the cereal and before its ravages could be stopped it destroyed the better part of said grain, thus making flour scarce and greatly raised in price.

PHILIP. When the Margrave sees this he will immediately annul his decree against importation.

BARON S. Certainly my dear Prince. But we will parry that. We will convince him by false statements that it will be better to try and conceal our condition as long as we can) from our Continental Brothers, lest avaricious men take advantage of our necessity. That the best thing to do will be to allow Levi the privilege of alone importing before the repeal takes general effect, the length of said privilege to be left to the discretion of the Finance Minister. Now, you see Levi can well afford to be liberal, backed up in this fashion. The immense amount of grain which he now has on hand will bring him in a tremendous revenue. After he hath disposed of what he now has he can import in such a manner as to make a good percentage for all concerned. When we think we have burdened the people as long as we dare, we will abolish his privilege. The whole plan is now laid bare to thee, my Lord.

PHILIP. A well-schemed plan. What's about the length of time requisite for a Finance officer to be in his berth before he can get wealth for himself and gold for his Patron?

BARON S. Well -if he's thoroughgoing and watchful after the first twelve months have become as things of the past, he may commence to feather his nest, and put by something handsome for his backer. You see, my Lord, he is first forced to pay strict attention to the duties of his office, in order to be able afterwards to reap a harvest. To cut a long story short, sir Prince, he must first make sure of his latitude before it's plain sailing.

PHILIP. Then, if the Margrave wishes to have the State faithfully and honestly served, he should remove the presiding officer of Finance from his station, and place a new one in his chair every twelfth moon.

BARON S. My Lord, I can swear that ever since Baron Von Dietz and myself have held sway o'er the exchequer the Margrave's *Purse* hath been full—always full—aye, packed.

PHILIP. I doubt thee not. Yet if Ethelbert knew the manner by which its bulk was increased, or kept plethoric, he'd strangle thee As thou hast said, Ethelbert loves the people. He takes more pride in doing right than the wearing of the title of Margrave. Sir, thou art a plunderer. The Minister of Finance and thyself make up a sum of knavish qualities that in two other monsters could not be found. (Raising his eyes, stretches forth his hands.) Oh, God! What a scourge to humanity are such vermin as these

BARON S. Now, my Lord, this is rude, most bitter language. Have not we done all that's possible for thee.

PHILIP. Sir Baron, thou shouldst have more lenity—more justice for the people.

BARON S. My Lord, your highness does not grapple properly with the subject, thou dost not understand thine own rights. The people we serve are the powers at court. Outside of the nobility, well, for mere mention we'll say the gentry, too, I hold the State but as the private property of its ruler. The people necessary only as they augment his pleasures. (Bowes.) Have we the honor to lift the weight of debt from off your Highness.

PHILIP. Thou wouldst know my answer? Well, then hark ye. No! a thousand times, no! Not at the expense of the good citizens of Baden.

BARON S. Well, I shall not consider this thy final answer. I shall interview thy Lordship again about this subject, for I feel most certain that ye will change thy mind after ye have pondered a bit.

PHILIP. Baron, thou art too kind. Thou art exceedingly polite. 'Tis a shame to spoil thy little game, yet mark me, sir, I shall obey the law and do my duty, and woe unto thee if thou dost not the same. Leave me, and remember what I've said.

BARON S. But, sir—

PHILIP. Leave, miscreant, do as I bid thee. I wish that all such plotting hounds as thou art were at the bottom of the ocean, along with their infernal schemes. Leave me, I say, and take this with thee to chew upon :—That if thou dost not act according to the legal sanctionings of thine office, and also immediately lower the tax on grain, and cease while Treasurer to have ought to do with the usurer Levi, or any men of the same calibre, I shall whisper in the ear of Ethelbert such a tale that shall make a flaming furnace a cooler place for thee than Baden. Go, before I throttle thee. (Stamping foot.) Go!

Exit Baron Stamwitz, C. through conservatory in haste

PHILIP. So this is the way our national Finance is managed. This, I suppose, is political economy,

These are the kind of men who cast the shadow of doubt on many a good and well-intending ruler. 'Tis strange so wise and observing a man as Ethelbert hath not measured yet these whelps, even though they've enjoyed their present dignities but six short months. Come, Philip, I think the best think for thee to do, is to get out of this Palace as soon as possible lest that terrible Duke essays to break thy back.

Enter Henrique Moritz L. just as Philip is about to exit L. They both come in contact.

HENRIQUE. MORITZ Prince Julien, at last. Well, I'm heartily glad of it for tired I am of hunting for thee.   I saw your Grace enter here with a Brahmin. I saw you from one of the Palace windows.   I was surprised at not having been warned of thy return. Oh, your Highness, but I've good news—merry news for thee.

PHILIP.   I must know who thou art, sir Mask, before I will hold converse with thee.

HENRIQUE.   I am Henrique Moritz. (Bows.) Your Highness's confidential page, I've merry news for thine ears. (Leads Philip down stage.) Oh, Prince, that elegant set of jewelry you sent to the beautiful opera singer, Del Rinaldo, did the business—worked like a charm, the enchanting actress surrenders at such a summons.   My Lord, she requested me to bring thee to her arms as soon as possible, that she might thank thee with the warmth of her love.   Art thou ready, Prince?

PHILIP.   No, fellow, no.

HENRIQUE.   What, dost thou not intend to go?

PHILIP.   Just so, my man.   Not one step will I take that leads towards her residence.

HENRIQUE.   But the Lady will expect thee.   My Lord, sir, it cannot be possible that thou art anxious to be rid of her.   Come, let me conduct thee to her presence.   She will weary of waiting.   'Tis not genteel to treat a Lady's love so lightly, especially after acting so deeply enamoured.

PHILIP.   Let her wait.   'Twill do her a world of good.   'Twill teach her to be patient.   Patience is rated among the virtues of mankind.   'Tis therefore worth possessing.

HENRIQUE· But, my Lord, you'll lose her. She will resent this coldness of thine most bitterly. Thou dost forget that Del Rinaldo is the most petted actress in Europe. Why, sir, people actually fawn about her. But, pshaw, all this is stale news to your Highness. Yet though she loves thee, beware, for remember she hath Spanish blood.

PHILIP. Let her resent it if she chooses so to do, I care not. For the present she can enliven the monotony of her vigil by warbling with her sweet, melodious voice, some lovesick ditty, or have her tire-woman rehearse her in her coming part. I'll not go to the "Andalusian," but the "Andalusian" can go to the Devil.

HENRIQUE. Why, Prince, hast thou really altered thy mind? Well, I comprehend thee not, my Lord, sir, for the last three months hast thou been sighing constantly for this identical opportunity, and now that it's arrived, thou art translated suddenly into an ice-berg. Surely this is arrant nonsense. What can have moved thee to this course.

PHILIP. Let this suffice : The change is my business, not thine.

HENRIQUE. Aha! perhaps thou hast other fish to fry ; per—

PHILIP. Presumest thou so. Well, what then ?

HENRIQUE. Perhaps a "Petit Soupèr"* with the Honorable Miss Witherspoon. But, let me warn thee, Sir Prince, (though her beauty and extreme loveliness of manner may charm thee as it must all men who are fortunate enough to possess her acquaintance.) that it would be dangerous to attempt anything dishonorable with her, for her family's one of the most wealthy, powerful and illustrious in all the British Empire. Her father (the Ambassador) is very devout, and—

PHILIP. I suppose the daughter is, too ?

HENRIQUE. 'Tis so asserted, my Lord.

PHILIP Well, be the lady what she may, I'm not seeking the Scotch beauty either with good or evil intentions. As for the Spaniard, she can do as thou hast said of me, sigh, sigh a little on her own account. Mark me, I break with her entirely, and so long as thou art

---

* F. a little supper.

my page, and value the keeping of my friendship, never presume to speak of that Iberian devil again.

HENRIQUE.   Oh, my Lord, but she's a very " Harem Queen," With one exception she's the most beautiful woman that ever these optics of mine has had the pleasure of beholding.   Yet, sir, since ye wish it, I'll never mention her again to your Highness.   Prince, now that I read thy mind a bit this much will I venture to say ;   That, though the Spanish girl is a poet's dream in form and feature, yet she is to imperious. I 'm sure, to suit thee rightly.   I'll wager a month's salary and all the perquisites of mine office for the same length of time, that your grace would have become disgusted with her ladyship inside of one short month of love.   If she had her deserts she—

PHILIP.   (Aside.)   I'm of the opinion that a severe castigation would greatly improve the quality of this royal page.   Black at heart is he, callous and full of festering schemes—a sort of intellectual devil.   For though base I do perceive much shrewdness beaming from his serpent eyes.   Not a fit companion for the son of Ethelbert the just.   Such a man is a stumbling block to any reformation in the character of so wayward a boy as Lord Julien.   'Tis a shame that the Prince (who I'm convinced is not really bad hearted,) is so plastic and malleable in the hands of knavish men.   (Aloud.)   Deserts in this world, Henrique, are bestown by Fortune with a crooked hand, else many a worthy beggar would be a ruler, and many a ruler an unworthy beggar.

HENRIQUE.   Aye, most veritably dost thou speak, my Lord, for I have discovered a girl—oh, such a lovely maid !   (Smacks lips.)   There's not another in Baden or anywhere else that'll compare with her, I'm certain, she's the exception I mentioned a moment ago to the " Andalusian."   I would be foolish, Prince, to attempt to describe her.   All that I can say is she's a very " goddess "—such hair—such eyes—such charms-- uhm, why, Prince, thou'll go mad on beholding her. She's only a peasant girl, my Lord.   It grieves me to see such an angel abiding in the obscurity of a cottage, to be mated and embraced some day by some unpolished and common man.   A fate that it's your grace's duty to avert by capturing her for thyself.   Such a mistress as she will make, your Highness has ne'er known.

PHILIP. (Aside.) By St. Peter but the fellow's surely speaking of my Rose, for there's no other woman in Baden that reaches this description (Aloud.) So thou dost conceive (if I'm to judge from thy language) that Julien can easily possess himself of this seraph in the entirety. Damn me if I argue with thee !

HENRIQUE. Saving your presence I say a fig for such talk. Julien of Baden needs no assurance from me. A grisette—a mere grisette—standing proof against the offers of a Prince—a Prince's love. Fie, my Lord, thou dost but jest. I've found out by watching the place carefully that a certain young yeoman (as splendid a specimen of manhood as she is of womanhood) is her lover. Yet that amounts to nothing, sir, for a little money and a snug berth would soon cause him to relinquish all claim to this "Hebe." She's the essence of artlessness, innocence and native grace. Thou shouldst see her as soon as possible.

PHILIP. And what method wouldst thou adopt to bring about such an issue safely and expeditiously.

HENRIQUE. Listen : Pretend that thou art a man of letters—a poet, aye, the bard's the very character—the very best one, thou, my Lord, can assume, because (grinning) because thou canst grind out a verse if thou art put to it. And if it's doggerel, as most of your Highness's poems are, it will matter little, for I'm sure she'll be but a poor judge. She'll think thou art the greatest of bards, and fall in love with thee for thy verse alone. Yet to make surety doubly sure, thou canst be a little lavish, you know, a sort of philanthropist. Of course, the first thing to be done is to obtain board at the cottage—a thing, I presume, very easy to do, as they are poor, and therefore want money—watch every opportunity to do them kindness without their suspecting that thou art studying so to do, and in a short space of time thou wilt be highly esteemed by them. When this juncture arrives thou canst consider thy plans have arranged themselves in proper shape, and—well I leave the rest to thine eloquence, rank and the magic which gold contains.

PHILIP. But what if this lover of hers will not accept a bribe. What if he should turn out one of those bold yeomen who knows the law, and understands his right, furthermore, is not afraid to defend then. What then ?

HENRIQUE. My dear Prince. I'm of the opinion
that the safest way to deal with the lout, is not to
give him an opportunity to prove rebellious. In other
words I'll have him kidnapped and placed in the army.
If he's a proud spirit there's the place to have it
tamed. This will afford him a chance to serve his
country, as every hound like him should be made to
do. I said he's good-looking (this yeoman), but who
the devil cares about the looks of a Plebeian. My
Lord, this lovely cottager is beyond doubt the most
bewitching creature that ever I ran down for your
Highness.

PHILIP. (With great excitement.) Where lives
she? Her name? her name, man? Out with it! Out
with it!

HENRIQUE. She resides in a lane that leads to
" St. Gregory's " Cathedral. She's the daughter of an
old /soldier who was killed in battle. Her mother is
Widow Marbury; her name is Rose.

PHILIP. (Seizing Henrique.) Of all the plagues
that doth afflict poor human nature there's not one
more to be dreaded than men like thee. (Hurls Henrique to the floor.) Fly, wretch, lest in my anger I do
thee harm. Dost thou not observe I'm greatly moved.

HENRIQUE. (Arising and bowing.) Sir, I do
perceive thou art displeased. Yet does the cause remain so hidden that I cannot divine the wherefore. I
always endeavored—

PHILIP. Ye guardian-angels, I thank thee for
the service rendered me. For surely what hath befallen me this night must be thy handy work. Oh, Rose!
Rose, my darling! What a snare hath been hatched to
entrap thine innocence.

HENRIQUE (Bowing,) Your pardon, my Lord.
But it seems that this pretty *wench* (I mean this lovely
maid) is not a stranger to your Highness. and that ye
love her too fondly for thy rank's good profit. Now,
how was I to know this—ye held it such a secret. How
was I to know, when I *ceased* to have your grace's confidence? It were better—

PHILIP. For thee, if distance ye put between us,
for I tell thee I'm in no mood to bear with thee.
Away! thou crooked soul'd conscienceless miscreant,
and take this with thee—yea, mark it well, that if ever

within a mile's proximity to the home of this young girl—to the roof made sacred by the hallowed presence of this sweet innocence I find thy loathsome visage I'll throttle thee on. the spot. By all that's holy I swear I'll keep my word.

HENRIQUE. But, my Lord, I only--

PHILIP. Leave me, I say, for though not splenetic, yet wear I that within my breast that makes me dangerous when I am wronged. Go, before I kill thee!

Exit L, Henrique, moodily.

PHILIP (Passionately.) Is honor dead, or fled to hearts of savage beasts? Why does Heaven permit such reptiles as this Henrique to stand erect and wear the form of man—wear it but to disgrace it. Oh, ye gods, can such a creature ever have felt the pure and endearing influences of home ? No- oh, no. If such had been the case the thought of that home woulds unnerve him when he aimed a blow (like which he pointed towards my Rose,) and which strikes, not at the character of woman singly, but offers insult to his own family ; his sisters who shared with him the hearth ; the mother who joyfully suffered that he might live. He can be naught else than some ghoul—a nest of sin deputied by some evil power to prey upon society. .Tis nothing strange that Julien hath become tainted by contact with such a human—no, I mean inhuman monster, as this court-page. The Prince is too easily lead for his own benefit. How all this escapes the watchful eye of the Margrave, is more than I can understand.

Enter Col. Bloomingdale R. on a run.   Rushes to Philip and seizes him by the arm.

COL. B, (Excitedly.) I'm here again, my Lord, I come to tell thee to fly. Prince Herman is now on thy track—he's coming this way as fast as his legs will convey him. It will not be well to cross his path just now ; he's in the worst of ill-humor,

Exit Col. Bloomingdale L. pulling Philip after him, just as Prince Herman enters C. from conservatory.

PRINCE HERMAN. (Drawing and brandishing a sword.) Dogs! Devils ! Stop, I say ! Think not to elude me, cowards ! Ye dare not face me ! Ye have hearts of hares ! By St. Paul but ye shall not escape me thus ; my blood is up ; I shall be avenged !

Exit Prince Herman L. in haste.

THIRD SCENE.

Scene.—A street front, perspectiveview. Enter Philip and Col. Blo. wingdale R. Both out of breath.

COL. B. My dear Julien, I think we have escaped the old hornet for the present. I'm surprised your Highness can run so well and appear so unwearied. I could never have imagined it possible, as ye take so little real exercise. I'll wager I m the most tired of the two.

PHILIP. Leave me, Bloomingdale, leave me. I will run no further. See, here comes Herman at the top of his speed.

COL. B. Aye, Prince, now do I myself behold him. You ask me to leave thee. That I shall not do. No, not while Herman carries a drawn sword, and wears upon his face the look of a wild beast hunting for prey. Besides, old Herman is one of the best of swordsmen.

PHILIP. Nevertheless, my friend, I say it will be better for both of us if I meet Herman alone. Therefore, I request thee to leave me. Furthermore, ye need have no fear as to my being seriously harmed, I'm quite familiar with the sword myself. I'd have thee remember. But if I were not, he would not dare to injure me too badly. Thou dost forget he's now in Baden, and not in Saxony.

COL. B. Well, have thy way, my Lord, I'll leave thee. Yet shall I not be afar, so if thou shouldst require me thou hast but to call. I go, your Highness, but much against my will.

Exit, Col. Bloomingdale, L. just in time to avoid being seen by Prince Herman, who rushes in R. with sword still drawn.

PRINCE H. Sir, I would speak a word or two with thee, if thou hast the courage to stay and give ear.

PHILIP. Speak, Sir, a hundred words if ye like, but more than this I will not grant thee. My time is limited, so let despatch be thy motto.

PRINCE H. Be not alarmed, I shall be most exceedinglybrief. Thou hast wronged me, deny it not. See, (tears off mask) I am Prince Herman, Duke of Chemnitz. I demand satisfaction. We are alone and armed—come, defend thyself. (puts himself in the attitude of attack.) Surely this is brief enough, I hope.

Philip now prepares for defense, yet retreats a step or two.

PHILIP. 'Tis sir, brief enough in words—almost a philological famine.

PRINCE H. [Coming forward.] Damn me, but it shall be brief enough in deed, as well.

PHILIP. [Retreating] Sir: art thou aware with whom thou wouldst seek to quarrel.

PRINCE H. Aye. Prince Julien (for thou art he), I am, you see, fully aware to whom I'm indebted for the shameful treatment I received at the Confectioners. I know the whole scheme of which I was made the victim. Come—talk less and give me a chance for satisfaction. If thou dost not grant me this, thou shalt be exposed to thy Royal Father—I shall demand of his liege ——

PHILIP. To carefully peruse the document to which thou didst attach thy Sign-manual, after taking oath to adhere strictly to the intent of said document—I mean the agreement between thyself and the Confectioner's Daughter. By-the-way, I'm in luck—I have it now in the breast-pocket of my vest.

PRINCE H. Pshaw—the Margrave would but smile at such a paper. Thou canst not hope with that document to do me much harm. Surely a nobleman may do as he pleases with a plebeian girl. Show (if thou so wouldst like this paper, not only to his Liege, but all the Court, for aught I care. [Aside.] Damn me, but he has me on the hip. [Aloud.] 'Twas a mere art of foolery, done when elated with mine—a bit of a lark. Fie, His Excellency will comprehend it all as readily, as I now read thy treachery.

PHILIP. Come then ; let's tarry here no longer; 'twold be a sin to waste more precious time ; let's lay the case before the Margrave.

PRINCE H. [Aside.] Curse him ; but he has me in his power. [Aloud.] No, I have concluded to settle it by the sword. To brand thee with ugly scars ; to mar that face which is thy pride. Oh ! how I hate thee, thou beautiful fiend.

Prince Herman now rushes furiously at Philip. A fight ensues, in which Prince Herman is wounded slightly, and his sword knocked from his grasp.

PHILIP. Sir grey-beard, I hope thou art satisfied. As for myself, I am more than satisfied.

PRINCE H. [Binding his left hand with hand-kerchief.] Sir—yet hope I to be avenged on Prince Julien. Think ye that because——

PHILIP. Behold then [Unmasks.] no emnity thy heart for me contains. See ; I am not Prince Julien. [Bows.] Sir : I bid thee adieu.

[Exit Philip. L.]

THIRD ACT, FIRST SCENE.

Scene.—Office of Duke Von Brunswick, Chief of Police (in the Citadel) Lieutenant Reber seated at a desk. L. Doors in flats R. and L. Sentries R. and L. passing to and fro. A Watchman guarded by a Gens D'Arme. Both standing before Lieutenant's Desk.

LIEUTENANT REBER. What, another Watchman ? Have they all gone crazy. Guardsman make thy change.

FIRST GENS D'ARME. [Saluting.] Mr. Lieu-tenant. This man was caught in the act of singing libellous songs, and creating disturbances.

FIRST WATCHMAN. [Saluting.] Good Mr. Lieu-tenant ; may it please your Honor, I ——

LIEUT. R. Take him below. See that he's securely locked in his cell by the Turnkey. [Aside.] By St. Michael ; 'tis growing serious—actually serious.

[Exit Gens D'Arme through R. D. in F. followed by Watchman, with bowed head, just as Captain Wetzelburgh and Col. Del Buchardo, enter R. arm-in arm.

LIEUT. R. [Saluting.] Ah Captain, thou hast arrived most opportunely.

CAPT. WETZELBURGH. Lieutenant ; inform the Chief I am the bearer of grave news. Tell him I must see him immediately, one of our men hath acted most unbecomingly in the presence of this Noble Gentleman In fact an insult this night he has received from a mem-ber of our force.

LIEUT. R. Was he of the Civic, or Military Po-lice ?

CAPT. W. Of the Third Division ; therefore of the Watch.

LIEUT. R. A Watchman. Well Captain, it's my opinion the Watchmen are all possessed to-night. Why I have consigned ten or twelve of them to the tender mercy of a cell-respectively.

[Exit Lieutenant Reber through L. D. in F.]

CAPT. W. [Looking R.] Bring in the prisoner.

[Enter R. A Watchman guarded by a Gens D'Arme, just as the Chief of Police enters (followed by Lieutenant Reber). Through L. D. in F. The Captain and Col. salute. Chief returns salutes.]

CAPT. W. A lively shape things now are taking, your Grace.

DUKE VON BRUNSWICK. Gentlemen : Lieutenant Reber hath informed me of what has transpired, but I must confess that it's astounded I'm beginning to be. The office of Chief of Police I have held full many a year ; yet in the whole course of my Superintendent-ship, never before the like of this night have I beheld. Surely the Watchmen have either gone mad, or con-cocted some base conspiracy. Thou canst depend upon it that I shall now begin to sift things to the bottom We have a number of Watchmen now in custody, one whose vile verses caused quite a difficulty between the Town's people and some of the National troops. Lieu-tenant Broadsword, of the Lancers, was very roughly handled, as were several other persons.

CAPT W. The devil fly away with all poets, says I.

DUKE VON B. [To Col. Del Buchardo.] Sir Colonel, for such I perceive thou art, wilt thou be so kind as to particularize the complaint, and make thy charge in person. This Watchman (I suppose) is the very man who dared offer insult to your worship.

COL. DEL BUCHARDO. Insult—I should say so. [Excitedly.] The low born knave hath not only in-sulted me but all who wear the uniform of a soldier. Sir : if I had given way to the passion that then surged within my breast, I should have smote him with my sword. [Shakes his riding whip and strides up and down a couple of times, exclaiming the while.] Wretch --his accursed verses rankles in my brain still. Why, gentlemen, it's an outrage. .

CAPT. W. Though I ordered the man's arrest, I did not hear the notes to which he tuned his tongue ; I was too far off to catch the words of his song. Colonel I prithee repeat them if it be possible.

DUKE VON B. Yes Col., repeat them—repeat the verses.

COL. DEL B. I'm sorry to say, I could not cor-rectly do so. But stay ; this Gen d'Arme overheard the song ; he was but across the street. He may re-member them.

DUKE VON B. [To Gen d'Arme.] Didst thou
catch the song my man.

SECOND GEN D'ARME. [Saluting] Your Honor ;
I can either sing it or speak it—just as it suits thee, I
have it all here. [touches his forehead.] Every word
sir.

DUKE VON B Sing it my man ; sing it, every
particle.

SEC. GEN. D'A. :

Bright feathers and plumes that tower above,
   Embroidered hats and uniforms of gold,
Waists strapped slim, and padded breasts,
   Such are our soldiers bold.

Chorus :—Oft an ass's hand doth clasp,
      A General's baton within its grasp.

A powdered wig and trailing queue,
   Occupation — cards, dancing and flirting too,
Empty heads, if their blood be blue,
   Will here far outstrip the good and true.

Chorus : Oft an ass's hand doth clasp,
   A General's baton within its grasp.

That's it to the letter, your grace.

COL. DEL B.   The identical song, word for word,
gentlemen.

SECOND WATCHMAN. (Saluting.) Good Sirs,
in all the days of my life, never did I a poetical verse
compose.

COL. DEL B.   Rascal, darest thou deny the singing of those infamous lines ? Darest thou deny that as
I was walking on thy beat, ye sang them in my hearing? Taking to thy heels as soon as ye perceived Captain Wetzelburgh and his guard.

SECOND WATCH.   Nothing do I know of all this,
upon my word I swear, most noble gentleman.

CAPT. W.   Why took thee to thy heels so swiftly
then ?

SECOND WATCH   I did not take to my heels, Sir
Captain.   A man passed me at great speed, as if pur-
sued, but I never left my beat.   I was about making
up my mind to give chase also, when I was seized and
informed that at the office of the Chief my presence was

required. I asked for what, I was told for unnecessary insolence to a gentleman of high standing. I was too far off either to hear or know the singing or when your hon-appeared upon the scene. This, gentlemen, is all I know of the affair.

COL. DEL B. I hope, Sir Chief, that your grace will lock the villain up, and severely punish him. I think it will have a tendency to bring him to his senses, (aside) and may, perhaps, be the instrumentality of causing him to divulge who are his accomplices. By dealing sternly with this knave, we may arrive at a better understanding of the whole plot, for plot I believe it is, and a dangerous one too.

DUKE VON B. I agree with your worship. I shall do as thou hast advised. I shall forthwith set the entire force on the lookout, offering a large reward, with promotion; this bait, I think, will do the business. Ah, I said the entire force, but that I can not do, for it's only the first and second divisions it seem that can be trusted, at present. Our force is divided into three divisions —the first are the Gens d'Armes, the second are the Police proper, and the Watch constitute the third. It will require the first and second sections to keep the third (who are no doubt backed by disaffected citizens,) still and compel these disturbers of the peace to respect law and order.

Enter a Corporal of Gens d'Armes R. Salutes.

CAPT. W. What now? Another Port I'll wager my epaulets.

CORPORAL. [To Captain], Noble Sir, Sergeant Siglitz having arrested the Captive, whom I have without, commanded me to bring him here immediately that they might be put under lock and key. I await your honor's orders.

CAPT. W. [To Chief.] Does your Grace wish to behold them, or shall I order them straight to confinement?

DUKE VON B. I would see them first. Let them be brought before me.

CAPT. W. Produce the prisoners, Corporal.

Exit Corporal R. Re-entering R, followed by several watchmen, guarded by Gens d'Armes, with guns.

DUKE VON B. These are the culprits. Hast thou any special charge to make Corporal.

COR.   Yes, your honor; for though they have all
disturbed the peace of good citizens, there's a couple I
thiuk need particular attention, two who've behaved
most villainously.   The first one sang a song under the
windows of the Palace of the Minister of Foreign Affairs, in which he said that the affairs of the Minister's
office were the affairs to which he was the most toreign.

THIRD WATCHMAN.   Your Grace.I cannot raise a
note.   In all my life of two score years I was never
known to sing a song.   Why. my lord, it's impossible
to fasten the singing of a song on me. Ye might as well
arrest a bull-frog as myself.

DUKE VON B.   Silence, thou miscreant. [To Corporal.]   What said the other knave, good Corporal.

COR.   He sang before the Palace of Bishop Pauls-
dorf that the " Lights of the Church " were in tallow no
ways wanting, though they yielded entirely more soot
and smoke than brilliancy of illumination.

DUKE VON B.   This is worse still.   [To prisoner.]
Were I the Margrave, I'd have thy tongue torn out for
daring to utter such blasphemy.   [To Captain]   Wetzelburgh, I shall hold thee responsible for the safety of
the prisoners.

CAPT. W.   Lieutenant Reber, see that the prisoners are confined each in a strong cell. and heavily iron-
ed.   Double the guard about the Castle.

Exit all.   Lieutenant Reber and Gens d'Armes with prisoners through R.
R door in F,   Captain Wetzelburgh, Col. Dal Buchardo and Duke von Brunswick L.   The Captain, Colonel and the Duke talking in dumb shows at once,
as tke Flats close in, etc.

SECOND SCENE.

SCENE.—A front perspective view,   (Street).   Enter Florence Stover R
leading a little (of some thaee summers) by the hand.   The mother sobs.

IDA STOVER.   Don't ky any more, mamma, tause
it makes me feel so ossal bad to see ou eep so.

FLORENCE STOVER·   [Kneeling and embracing
child C.]   O God,God, pity me, have mercy Heaven !
Yet, if it be Thy will that I must suffer, Oh pity, for
virtue's sake, this,my precious one; for him crucified, be
merciful to this helpless, this innocent child· Father Almighty, Thou fountain head of this great universe, to
thee I pray! Oh, take my darling, take her to that happy land where all is peace and love. Take her, ere cankered crime enfolds her in his pestilential embrace, and
brands her with his damnate kiss.

IDA. 'Ill mamma be 'ere too, in ee sky, in heaven wiz her 'ittle Ida?

FLOR. I hope so, my darling. I hope such will be the will of Him before whom all hearts lie bare.

IDA. 'Ell her' ould do ite er way. Her 'ould'nt 'tay er monent. No, not wizout her mamma.

FLOR. (Musingly.) Shall I do it? Shall I give heed to the tempter? Shall I take upon myself the authority of ridding me and mine from the gloomy channel in which our lives so roughly groove? Yes! No! Yes! oh yes, it must be done. But stay—is it a crime? No, no, 'tis not a crime to fly from a living hell; to exterminate one's life when that life hath ceased to be aught save a burden, a weary burden, crushing thee, as it were, to the earth. I will do the deed. The Bible itself vindicates the act I'm about to perform, saying, " If thy hand offends thee, cut it off; if thine eye offends thee, pluck it out." My life offends me, therefore I take it. Aye, thus end all the trials of myself and daughter. [To Ida.] Darling, let thy speech follow mine in prayer, and may the Great Jehovah hearken unto our petition. [Draws dagger.]

Enter Myriam Isaacs R. Seizes Florence's hand, and takes away the dagger forcibly. Florence rises, and draws her child towards her.

FLOR. [Excitedly] How darest thou interfere with me? Who art thou? Give me back my weapon. Give it back, I say, lest, like some ravenous beast I do thee fearful injury.

MYRIAM ISAACS. Thou would'st know me; well let it suffice that a frien l am I to thee. Madame, I would save thee, to live and bless thy home.

FLOR. Woman, I have no home, no home save where the angels dwell, that is if one like me dare think of Heaven in such a fashion. Give me back my knife, and with its keen and trusty edge let me unloose my soul, that it may wing itself unto the awful presence of the Almighty. My cross is too heavy for me, and I can no longer stagger under its burden. I tell thee I must die, there's no escape. [Points to child.] We must die.— Large as is the earth, there's no place where we can abide beyond the reach of pain, penury and despair. 'Tis said that the way of the transgressor is hard, and that those who sin must suffer, yet if this be the law of Providence, why does society take the libertine smiling-

ly by the hand, scorning and loathing the poor creature
whose ruin he caused, whose greatest fault was that
she loved too wildly —too confidingly. Oh! man where
is thy constancy! Oh, woman, on whom canst thou
depend for sincere affection, for truth and love. Return my knife, I say, I wish no further parley.

MYRIAM. The latter part of thy speech I do accord thee true, as all must who are observing. With no
arrogance I use the personal pronoun I, for I have suffered, and those who have worn a sorrow in their
breast, have known misery, felt the touch of dark-
browed vice, can better understand and I here make
mention that when e're it's necessary that man should
sit in judgement on his fellow man, that they alone
who've suffered shouldst occupy the throne of justice—
the judgment seat. Friend, though I acknowledge the
force thy words contain, yet do they not appertain to
thee, for thou art wedded ; thy child beside thee is legal
as the law.

FLORENCE. Ly the stars above us I swear my
daughter is the fruit of holy wedlock. Yet what signifies her legitimacy if her father conceives her not— that
is, thinks his wife unchaste, her offspring unlawful--what
if some '' human '' Katie Dids '' come forward with the
cry of, 'tis false, 'tis true. Aye, and those proclaim-
ing 'tis false, preponderating. What then ? Is not the
happiness of my home forever fled, does the difference
between 'tis false, 'tis true, lessen the agony of the
troubled heart, (especially when the possessor of that
heart knows that though her child is lawful, yet hath
she erred) will it narrow the breach—will it unite them
again in that delightful bond of love which Heaven,
through the church hath sanctified, and God himself ordained as the proper state of man ? No, it will not.
What, then, am I to—

MYRIAM. Thy pardon—but stop a moment, for I
wouldst tell thee that which to my mind will germinate
to more than a hope of reconciliation—a husband's
love, a happy united household.

FLORENCE. That ye mean well, I am convinced.
Yet I pray thee leave us alone with our sorrow. (Turns
to Ida.) Oh, my child !—my dear, dear child, why
must we die—die in the bloom of life ! Yet, 'tis writ-

ten—our fates are sealed. I cannot endure this life longer, and I dare not die and leave thee behind without
a mother's guidance and protection. The thought of
what ye might become maddens me. We are so poor,
so friendless. (To Myriam.) Madam, I beseech thee
to return my dagger.

*Myriam rushes L. and hurls the dagger away, returns hastily and throws
aside her vail. Florence screams and falls into Myriam's arms. Myriam then
kisses and caresses little Ida.*

MYRIAM. (Disengaging herself.) Ah, Florence,
few are the numbers of our joys, and fewer still are they
who can boast the possession of those joys unmixed
with the aqueous fluid that dwells in sorrow's eye Little did I think of being as I am—a wretched woman, or
of beholding thy sunny face bathed in tears.

FLORENCE. Dear Myriam, I thought thee dead.

MYRIAM. And thou, my friend, I thought were
happy, until recently. Yet, hark thee—for the hand of
destiny is in our meeting, I have that to tell thee which
I consider good news. Thy husband stops to-night at
the house of old Gottlieb Montagna ; haste ye and get
there before him, as, in my mind, it will service thee to
meet him under the roof of those worthy people. He
holds them (Gottlieb and his wife) in the greatest esteem. You was always a favorite of theirs. Go and
meet him there, and I'll wager thee it will all be well.

FLORENCE. Oh, would to Heaven that a reconciliation might take place if only for my child—my little
Ida. I shall follow thy advice, but not till thou hast
told me something of thyself, and in what manner my
troubles became known to thee.

MYRIAM Well, then. When I arrived at my
apartments last eve, I was surprised, on entering, by a
flood of light that streamed in from a knot hole in the
partition that divides our rooms. Now, as thy abode
had remained unoccupied ever since I domiciled in this
house, I thought I would see who was my companion
in misery (for none but the miserable dwell in this vicinity.) Imagine my amazement when I beheld thee.
Partly from thy conversation with little Ida, and partly
from letters which thou, after reading, apostrophised, I
gleaned thy tribulation, my first impulse was to make
myself known, but after mature deliberation I conceived
it better to remain incog. I rerobe, proceeded to thy

husband's intending to inform him of the wrong he was doing—an injustice to himself, his wife and child.   But I was foiled, for he was not at home.   Yet this very night I saw him—saw him enter the tavern of the " Red Dragon."   I dared not follow, but through the aid of a thaler, I procured an urchin who delivered my mess- age.   This was his answer :   (Reads.)

"STRANGER—That thou meanest well I am con- vinced.   Yet, that thou art deceived I am most certain. But if the person of whom ye speak needs money she hath but to send for it.   I stop. to-night, at old Gott- lieb's.   To-morrow night thou mayest bring her to my house ; I will grant her audience.   I will do anything that I can to prevent her and her child from starving, but nothing more.   She and I are one flesh no longer.

(*Signed*) LEOPOLD STOVER,

Yeoman."

You know all that I shall now reveal ; neither have I the time if I would, to tell thee more ; again I say, haste thee to the home of the Montagnas, and. if with their assistance, thy prayers and entreaties do not pre- vail, thy husband hath no heart, but in its place a lump of steel.   Leave me now, Florence, I prithee.   Thou hast no time to lose.   (Leads mother and daughter L.) I hope when next we meet all dismal nebulae with the shadowy past shall buried lie.

Florence and Myriam embrace.   Myriam kisses little Ida.   Florence and Ida then make exit L.

MYRIAM.   (Looking after them.)   Yes, for thee and thine there may still be happiness, but for me there's nothing left but the grave.   Well, I'll be content if be- fore I don my cerements, this (draws a knife) reaches the heart of Emil Valdmeyer.

Exit Myriam Isaacs R.

THIRD SCENE.

Scene—Full stage, St. Gregory's Cathedral in the background brilliantly lighted.   Clock strikes the hour of midnight (as the flats open) and the bell tolls slowly several times.   Enter Philip R. removes mask.

PHILIP.   Thank Heaven, the hour at last has come when I may put aside my royalty, and once more be Philip Montagna.

Enter Rose Marbury L.

ROSE.   Philip will soon be here, and then—

PHILIP.   (Crossing to Rose.)   Philip is here now. (Embraces her.)Yes, sweetest love, thy Philip is again beside thee, and for the privilege a thousand thanks to the powers above be rendered. May the Furies fly away with all courts and courtiers say I. Oh, how few among them are aught else than knaves—powdered, wigged, ribbon'd scoundrels.

ROSE. (Inclines head.) Listen, Philip! (Places fingers to mouth.) Sh—I think I hear music; I, sh—

As Rose begins speaking, the organ is very faintly heard. As she finishes it is distinctly heard, rising louder and louder, until it reaches full power, then gradually dies away.

ROSE. That was lovely, Philip.

PHILIP. Yes, Rose, 'twas exceedingly sweet. But let us harken, there's more to come.

The bell tolls thrice, then the organ bursts forth, accompanied by the priests chanting as follows :

PRIESTS. Great Jehovah, God of love,
Who rules above—who rules above
Look down with pity on us here,
Thou God whom we adore and fear.
Oh, with a smile our pathway cheer—
Our pathway cheer.
Chorus :—Amen, we sing,
      In the name of the Father and the Son,
      The Holy Ghost and blessed Virgin.
      Amen—Amen.
We thank thee for the year that's gone,
We praise thee—we praise thee for the one now born,
We kneel as sinners before Thy throne ;
Help us, Father, our sins atone ;
Oh, with a smile our pathway cheer—
Our pathway cheer.
Chorus .—Amen, we sing, etc., etc.

The priests having finished chanting, the organ slowly dies away. The bell tolls thrice, then the great doors swing open, the priests file out, the organ bursting forth again, plays until priests make exit R. I. E. Bell tolls thrice again, then the doors are slowly closed, and all grows dark within.

PHILIP. My sweet, my darling Little dream ye that this very night, on Transformation's fleet Hippogriff I've ridden. Been carried, as it were, into the lap of of Luxury, stood face to face with Pomp, hobnobbed with Power, and have born upon mine own shoulders the mantle of high authority. Oh, Rose, I have beheld—But, stay, some other and more propitious time I'll inform thee. Tell me, sweetest one—tell me that thy heart yearns for me, as mine does for thee.

ROSE. Philip, dear, that I do love thee, thou
knowest full well.   Methinks it more befitting, myself,
to ask whether thou dost love me—love me with honest
love.   Now that thou hast grown to be so great a man--
I mean a rich man--for there's no analogy between
money and true greatness.   Philip, thou wert always
great, a man possessed with a lofty o'ertopping mind is
a genius, and a genius, whether he inherits poverty or
wealth, whether his name is carved on marble, or
stamped upon the banner of fame, or dies unknown,
yet is he great In the latter case he lacks notoriety, 'tis
true (which 'I'm sorry to say is too oft mistaken for
greatness), yet is he great.   Such a man art thou,
Philip—a genius.   Mind is the gift and handiwork of
God ; money is but the tinkering of men on which only
sordid, narrow-visioned souls, alone set store.

PHILIP. 'Tis true that greatness is not of money;
'tis (as ye say,) too oft mere notoriety, aye, mere notoriety, strutting in false plumes and misnomered greatness.   Yet money in the hands of an ambitious person
may be made the stepping stone to fame.   But when ye
call me great, I am compelled, (though deeply sens·ble
of the compliment intended,) to say most emphatically
that thou dost err, for I feel, darling, as yet to that distinction I cannot lay just claim.

ROSE. 'Tis thyself that dost err, Philip, but for the
present have thy way.   To me, at least, thou art all
that's great, and I prognosticate (in spite of the poor
opinion thou hast of thy merits,)that the world will yet
talk loud of thee, and justly too, placing thy name (and
nicheing thee) with those who were born never to be
forgotten.

PHILIP. Well, Rose, for thy sake, I hope thou art
a true prophet, that Fate will one day contrive it as thou
hast predicted; yet know that all I ask of the Dispenser
of blessings is health, strength, a sound mind, a chance
to earnest an honest and comfortable living, and darling,
that thou shalt share that living with me, and be the mother of my children, my own, my paradise, my wife —
But how came thee to know that I have about my person a considerable sum of money, or rather, I should
say, its equivalent.

ROSE. Why, with thine own dear lips, Philip, didst
thou inform me of my wealth.   Ah, love, those whose

coffers are filled with the yellow dust, and who have never been poor, know not how thankful they should be
for the lucky associations of ‚circumstances that placed
them above want, above the many annoyances that poverty is heir to. Philip, how much is it altogether what
thou hast with tnee, and what thou didst leave with
me.

PHILIP. If I was not aware that nothing but the
purest German passed thy lips, I'd swear that thou hadst
been addressing me in a foreign tongue, (understand me
—I mean thy last utterance,)for not a word of what thou
hast just said do I with clearness take unto my comprehension. The money that I have, I got from a noble
high at court, but though in my possession, it belongs
me. Surely thou art jesting when thou sayest I gave
not to thee gold.

ROSE. Philip, Philip, hast thou been drinking?—
Thou art confounding sense. [Produces a purse]. Behold, is not my proof most tangible. Thou saidst thy ticket had carried off the prize. Oh, my heart is full—big
with joy. I've half a mind to give thee a good hugging.
[Replaces purse.] After this, I shall stand forth a champion of lottery, since through it we are both made happy.

PHILIP. Well, as to the hugging, if thou dost in-
sist upon it, of course I'll not object, but as to my having won at lottery, most sorrowfully I must say 'tis not
a fact, for my ticket (as it has ever been), was a blank.
Rose, I'm of the opinion, that those only are successful
who are interested in the concern. I'm no richer now
than I was when last we met. But tell me, darling, how
thou didst become possessed of the purse of gold which
in thine own sweet hands I did but just behold.

ROSE. (Piquantly.) Philip is trying to be very
funny, isn't he? Why this contradiction? With thine
own mouth, again I assert, thou didst so state as I have
spoken. and the purse of gold with thine own hands
placed thou into mine. I prithee, cease this nonsense;
'tis cruel to toy with those who love thee.

PHILIP. Rose, collect thyself, I do conjure. Call
up thy recollection to thine aid. Last night I told thee
if it were possible I would accompany thee to Matilda's, and spend there the evening; but if my father
should be taken with one of his attacks, I should be
necessitated to take his place on the watch. On going

home, I found him ill. I immediately sent thee a message, informing thee that I could not enjoy the gathering given by Matilda, or even escort thee there, but that I had arranged it with the Sergeant of the Post, through Corporal Vollensdorf, so that I would be relieved just before the clock of St. Gregory's struck the hour of twelve, and requested that thou wouldst meet me there exactly at the same time, which in the answer to my note (penned by thine own dear hand), the said request thou didst agree to comply with. Now, Rose, from the time I parted with thee at thy gate, up to the present moment, I have not beheld thy lovely face.

ROSE. (Suddenly.) Oh, Philip, how came I not to notice that thou art not dressed as a watchman.—What's that thou hast hanging to thine arm—a mask? Oh, Philip, Philip, where hast thou been. To some ball, I suppose—deceived me, deceived thine own trusting Rose. Oh, but this is too cruel. (Weeps). Who—who wouldst ever have — ever thought this of—of Philip— my Philip, Oh, my heart is breaking.

PHILIP. Rose, dearest, if thou wilt but be patient, I'll soon dispel thy sorrow.

ROSE. (Ceasing to weep.) Philip, if thou hast aught to say that will lift the weight from off my heart, I ask thee in heaven's name to speak it quickly.

PHILIP. My own sweet one, it shall be so. Now, dry thine eyes, and listen. Just as I had finished the first call of my watch, and was about thinking how happy I'd be by thy side, and the watch-duty at an end, I was suddenly accosted by a masked man, wearing the apparel thou now seest on me. The wearer asked me to exchange with him for the remainder of my watch. And as it was so bitter cold (at least, so it seemed to me), I consented, first exacting a promise from him that he would do nothing detrimental to the dignity of the office he briefly desired to be invested with I then took my departure, intending to seek the protection of some inviting tavern, and there, over a glass of old ale, in an enticing corner of the chimney, weave bright pictures of the future, in which you, darling, would have been the central figure. The stranger and I were to exchange a little before the time of thy coming, so that thyself and the Corporal's guard of relief should nothing know of our proceedings. The relief should be here now, I wonder what can have detained them. The city is quiet, so there's no need for extra duty being entailed upon any one. I wonder, too, why the Prince doth not put in his appearance. The Prince I speak of, Rose, is none other than Julien, the wayward son of our good Ethelbert.

ROSE. Prince Julien; didst thou say Prince Julien, Philip ?

PHILIP Aye, that I did. The gentleman with whom I exhanged was none other than he.

ROSE. Art thou sure Philip ? Art thou sure ?

PHILIP. As certain as that thou art the most charming of lovely girls, and the only woman (excepting my dear old mother) that I passionately adore.

ROSE. Aha—so then it was Julien I kissed, and who returned my kiss so fervently, and who gave me the gold I —

PHILIP. (Slightly aroused.) The sly dog, this is too much ; ye kissed Julien and he—

ROSE. Why Philip darling ; though Julien was the recipient of this voucher of sweet affection, it nevertheless was meant only for thee—there now don't be jealous, for thou knowest if Julien occupied a Ruler's Throne—aye, sat President to all the many Governments that comprise the dear land which we call Germany, instead of the Governor (son of a Sovereign over one exalted though that be) I would reject his suit, and favor thine.

PHILIP. (Kissing Rose.) Pardon sweetheart, pardon. I do believe thee, I do indeed, with all my heart I thank thee for the compliment—the honor thou dost confer on me. The dissatisfaction my language revealed was not caused by any act of thine, 'twas the audacity of the Prince, that vexed me. If Julien wishes to preserve a whole skin, and a sound body, he'd better not repeat this kissing business. Now Rose, to pay myself for the delight the thievish Prince robbed me of, I'm going to take a baker's dozen of kisses (which ye know is thirteen), so prepare (Embraces Rose.) Prepare thy tempting lips.

ROSE. Philip, be careful ; what if some of the relief should catch thee thus engaged. Thou wouldst be fined. Pshaw, I wish the naughty Prince would come, and the Corporal dismiss thee. Oh, dear, I fear something's wrong, Philip, I--

PRINCE JUL. (Excitedly.) In the name of all the gods at once, I prithee not to keep me waiting. There's no time, my lad to throw away : the officers of the law are out in full strength. the city's in great commotion. All this I suppose is news to the quiet state.

PHILIP. Let us re-exchange with all the haste we can. Then, I should not like to be found in thy establishment. Yet, as this is so quiet a place, I imagine we've nothing to fear, at least for the present.

Philip and Julien now exchange garments, each quickly redressing in his own. Music

PRINCE JUL. I promised thee a recompense (feels for purse), hang it but I--Ah, (observes Rose--bows,) good evening, excuse me for not noticing thee before. (To Philip.) Thy sweetheart has it, for it was to her I gave it a short time ago. Keep the gold, my friends, and consider it thine. Now. get thee gone, lest harm befall thee.

ROSE. We wish not thy gold, sir—(hands purse to Philip)— we wish not a dollar of thy money.

PHILIP. [Putting purse in Julien's hand.] Sir, we thank thee, yet we— that is I (from all I've seen and heard) advise thee to keep thy money, as I'm most convinced thou'll need all thy gold. (Produces a paper.) Take this also, it's an order drawn by the son of the Duke of Chemnitz—take it as it belongs to thee. Now, I think our business is at an end (Suddenly.) But stay, there's something more I'd say before we part, (turning towards Rose). Behold this innocent girl. She is my affianced bride--my soul's sweet comforter. I love her with a devotion unparalleled--I adore her. Now, mark me, if harm should befall her through thy machinations, I'd tear thy heart from out its socket. If thou shouldst even injure so much as one little hair of her dear head I'd trample thee in the dust, aye, and this I'd do if thou wert a thousand times Prince Julien.

PRINCE JUL. (Looking astonished.) Prince Julien--How comes it that thou dost know me, and by what strange chance obtained this order from Prince De Baldwin ? Really, I am amazed.

PHILIP. Let it suffice that thou hast been honestly dealt with, my Lord.

PRINCE JUL. Be not angered with me, friend. Yet I must confess, so lovely a woman is enough to make any one jealous. Young man, I like thee—I liked thee at first sight, and now that thou hast shown thyself mettlesome I like thee still the more. Now, come—tell me where and how thou didst obtain this paper, and how ye learned my name and title. (Places purse and paper in pocket.) Come, speak out, my lad.

PHILIP. I was taken for thee as I was passing Count Wortenburgh's mansion. His Lordship came out through a rear gate and headed me off, insisting that I should enter and make merry at the ball. I complied. General De Baldwin was there also. Mistaking me for thee, he gave me the order to pay, as he said, a gambling debt. He and her Ladyship his wife quit Carlsuhe this very night. They leave never to return to Baden again.

PRINCE JUL. Art thou a witch, or am I dreaming.

PHILIP. For the sake of thy good father I wish thou wert. The State Treasurer told me that if he and his cousin are kept in control of the national purse, they ll so manage it that your Highness will be most bountifully provided for. Both gentlemen agree that if your Grace will but use thine influence with the Margrave to arrange it so that thy Lordship shall not only fill thy pockets, but have the responsibility of the indebtedness to Sir Abraham Levi and the Goldsmith Brothers, lifted as it were from off thy noble shoulders. (Presents a purse.) Your Highness can give this to our friend the chamberlain with my compliments. He loaned it to me at the masquerade. I did not need it so therefore it is intact.

PRINCE JUL. (Accepting and stowing away purse.) Art thou a magician? Surely, thou art not a watchman! No, by St. Peter! No! Sir, what answer did ye render the Treasurer?

PHILIP. Well, your Honor. surrounding myself with proper dignity—I refused my consent. would'nt listen to the scoundrel. In fact I spurned the offer.

PRINCE JUL. (Wildly.) By the gods. what do I hear; refused thy consent, spurned the offer. Man—hath thy reason fled thee!

PHILIP. (Proudly.) No, but, such I fear, is the case with thee, my Lord, else wouldst thou have chosen more fitting companions. The actress whose luxurious form has been bewitching thee for this some time back. I have so fixed it that she'll henceforth hold thee in contempt. His Highness, Prince Herman, Duke of Chemnitz, swears vengeance 'gainst thee for the trick played him in the confectioner's cellar. I left him greatly exercised.

PRINCE JUL. Thou art Satan himself, thou canst be none other. Oh, would that I were out of this!

PHILIP. Sir, thou art mistaken. I lay no claim to such a distinction. The only devil here is your Highness.

PRINCE JUL. Oh, go to—and I am——·

PHILIP. In danger? Well, that remains for time to tell; yet, as for the Duke, I think he can be easily settled. That's if thou dost act with boldness, remember.

* * * * * *

> Boldness hath power and magic in it
> 'Tis the mail which genius puts on
> To make his arm more strong.
> And be the cause whate'er it may,
> Boldness alone can win it.

The Royal Duke was like a ship hit below her waterline, when I reminded him of the document he signed in relation to the confectioner's daughter, and threatened if he pressed too hard to place it where the Margrave's eye would fall upon it; so I presume he'll not trouble thy good father with thy misconduct But there is one thing that he will endeavor to do, and that is—provoke thee to a fight—a duel.

PRINCE JUL. In the name of all that's wonderful, I must confess that thou dost amaze me. How——

PHILIP. Waste no time in being amazed—but be on thy guard, for Herman is possessed of a terrible temper, and there's no telling what wild act he may perform. Thou wouldst like to know how I obtained the knowledge of this paper about the confectioner's daughter. Well—let this for the present suffice: through the same mysterious association of circumstances by which I learned all that I have told thee.

PRINCE JUL.   Since it seems that nothing is to thee a secret, wilt thou be so good as to inform me of the means by which Prince Herman gained his information.

PHILIP   Yes, certainly.   Through her Honor the Mayoress of Carlsruhe, who, by some strange chance, obtained thy secret, and holding thee in' great disfavor, divulged it to Herman of Chemnitz.

PRINCE JUL.   My good friend (for such I now believe thee), I thank thee for this information.   I also thank thee for the credit thou hast reflected upon me whilst acting in the capacity of Crown Prince of Baden. This latter expression of mine (to thee, no doubt,) must seem strange; yet, nevertheless, I mean sincerely what I've said.   'Tis true, at first I was vexed, for thou hast greatly interfered with my schemes.   But as I watch thee and see how much more lofty thy nature is than mine, how much better a Prince thou wouldst make than myself, I grow ashamed, doubly so when I call to mind the last promise I made my noble father to reform.   All of a sudden, my past life like an avalanche doth rush upon me, and I sicken at the shadow that it casts.

PHILIP.   My Lord, keep up thy spirits, for I believe there's hope for and stamina in one who desires to be better.   In spite of thy evil doings, I have not thought really ill of thee; 'tis thy base associates who are damning thee.   Throw them aside, they do but clog thy path to promotion in the ranks of true nobility.

PRINCE JUL.   Sir, thou art no petty observer, and are blessed with intelligence of more than the common Thou art calculated to lead, to walk, as it were, before thy fellow-men.   The poet. whose pen gave birth to the following, I'm inclined to think was a close student.

> A nation's pride is not the patrician
> Or a vast extent of soil,
> 'Tis her bold and virtuous middle class
> And her honest sons of toil.

But, friend, though acknowledging the wisdom of the bard, I cannot help conceiving thee something else than a watchman. [Smilingly.]   Yet don't imagine that I longer suspicion thee as being consanguineous with his Satanic Majesty

PHILIP.   Prince, to speak in unison with fact, I'm not a watchman, but simply a substitute for the man whose name I bear.   By rank, I am a yeoman; by occupation, a florist; by circumstances poor, I'm Philip, son of Gottlieb Montagna, the watchman.

PRINCE JUL. Montagna—I've heard that name before. Let me see—pshaw—I cannot seem to place it, yet it strikes me that I've heard my father mention it as belonging to a brave old soldier Comrade, give me thy hand, and thou, sweet lass, also give me thine.

Philip and Rose now each grasp one of Julien's hands—all come forward—C.

PRINCE JUL. Fair Maiden, and thou good Philip, listen: 'Tis no secret that I have ignobly conducted myself; that my father's loving heart I've greatly pained; that though my companions are—are, (well, as the phrase goes,) gentlemen, yet are they the most disreputable men in Baden. But though all this be true, I nevertheless feel in my breast an honest influence tugging away, as it were, to make itself felt, to free me from the toils of my evil genius. And friends, I think it hath succeeded. I seem now "alter-ego."* Let's leave this place with despatch, I fear we've tarried here too long already. I wish it strictly understood that, though we separate to night, yet are we to become better acquainted in the future.

Prince Julien now shakes hands with Philip, and kisses the hand of Rose. All essay to leave, but are stopped by Sergeant Seldner and his guard of Regulars, who've stealthily entered C—from behind Cathedral—after Julien led Philip and Rose down stage—They all start back amazed, on discovering the soldiers.

ROSE. [Clinging to Philip.] Oh, Philip, what shall we do? I fear we are drifting into trouble.

PHILIP. [Softly.] All will yet be well. Julien hath given his promise that no harm should befall me or mine, and I'm confident he's too proud to break his word, even to shield himself. Of course, he wishes to escape recognition, if possible.

PRINCE JUL. (Softly.) I'm very sorry that we're captured, yet have no fear, for I shall keep my promise. Carry a high head, and take no thought as to consequences.

SERGEANT SELDNER. Well, comrades. I hold we've yielded this party ample time for consideration, and to become aware of our presence. So now let some of you take into custody that handsome Watchman.—[Points to Philip.] Arrest that man.

---

* Another self.

Three soldiers rush forward—One pushes Rose aside, and relieves Philip of his staff, while the others each seize an arm·

PHILIP.   Sergeant, why this violence? By whose authority dost thou commit this act.

SERGEANT S.   By the authority of an order from my superior, Captain Von Desendorf, of the Margrave's staff.   He commanded me to arrest every watchman of whom I had any suspicion.   Now, as I entertain some doubts about thee, I've arrested thee.

PHILIP.   My good Sergeant, I'll not proceed one step until I behold the warrant for my arrest.   I have not broken the law. Furthermore, I am a watchman. Thou canst not arrest a private citizen without a warrant and a cause, much less a watchman.

SERGEANT S.   Hark ye.   Captain Von Diesendorf becoming aware of the disturbances going on here in the city, and ascertaining that the cause lay with the watch, commanded me to arrest every watchman who appeared at all suspicious.   But the Margrave, hearing of the trouble too, immediately issued orders that not only the suspicious ones, but every man wearing the uniform of a watchman should be arrested and put in the Castle.   Be it known to thee, an officer, whether commissioned or non-commissioned, in the immediate service of the Margrave, needs not a warrant to invest him with legal power to make arrests.   The law vouchsafes this as a right due to those whose duty it is to guard the person of the sovereign.   I was ordered to make arrests as quietly as possible, and with despatch.   The Margrave also armed me with a warrant, so as to prevent any watchman (who might erroneously consider the statutes), rebelling against my authority.   Now, as thou art not satisfied with my military prerogative [produces and unfolds a paper, with seals], and as I am desirous to take thee to jail in a peaceful manner, just cast thine eyes over this document [holds it before Philip, and no further parley wilt thou make.

Philip seizes paper, glances at it a second, then returns it to the Sergeant, who replaces it in his breast pocket.

PHILIP.   Well, as it appears that thou art privileged to arrest without a warrant, yet have one, why of course I must now consider myself absolutely thy prisoner.   Sergeant, thou art most potently armed.   Nevertheless, I've this to say in my defense, that no matter what crime hath been committed by any member of the watch, I am innocent

PRINCE JUL. [Pompously.] Weary not thy brain with troublesome thoughts. There's been no crime committed. I'll settle this business. [Aside]. I hope this bravado will dull the fierceness of this soldier. If so, Philip may be released and I escape detection.

SERGEANT. [Surveying the Prince.] Well, who art thou that's so cleverly trained in braggardism. My gay-feathered songster, I think I'll settle thee. Come, thou shalt keep company with the watchman. Secure him [pointing at Julien], secure this boaster,

Two soldiers rush upon Julien, each seizing an arm. He struggles, and frees himself. The Sergeant confronts him with drawn sword. The guards form a semi-circle. He is again pinioned. He yields.

PRINCE JUL Damn thee, and thy interfering hounds, I surrender. But——

ROSE. Oh, Sergeant, Sergeant, thou knowest not whom thou hast made prisoner. This gentleman is a great lord of the court. Thou hadst better set him at liberty.

PHILIP. Yes, thou hadst better liberate him, or harm may come to thee. He is——

PRINCE JUL. Stop, sir, stop, good Philip, expose me not. Let's accompany the Sergeant at once. I promise thee all will yet be well. [Aside.] If I must reveal my part in this night's frolic, I'd rather do so to the Minister of Police. Lucifer, but I have no churl to deal with in this Sergeant. [Aloud.] Come, Sergeant, I, or rather we, are ready. Move on.

SERGEANT S Thy little game won't work with me, my lads. I'm used to this kind of chaffing. I've often had fellows try to intimidate me with wind, pretending to possess both rank and power, endeavoring to frighten me with the idea that dire punishment awaited me if I lugged them in. But I always lugged them. I tell t heeI don't scare rappid, not a bit. I'm here to execute the law, and I am going to do my duty. Neither bribes nor fear shall deter me.

PHILIP. The young girl may retire, may she not, Sergeant?

SERGEANT S. The pretty maid here—well—yes, she may go. But stay—I'll just mark her face and take her address first, then she can leave as soon as she likes. [Produces book.] Where dost thou live, my lass?— [Scrutinizes Rose.] In what quarter of the town dost thou dwell?

PHILIP. She resides at No. 76, in——

SERGEANT S. Cease! Thy tongue's too ready. [To Rose.]Go on, I do await thee.

ROSE. Sir, I dwell in a cottage on the east side of a small lane, called Place Von Bruen, adjoining a carpenter shop. The number is 76. The Street or Place (I suppose you are aware,) is but a continuation of the great highway or lane of St. Gregory's. It owes existence to the park or playground that separates it from the lane proper. Its terminus is the lofty mill of Captain Pfrote. Good Sergeant, if thou wert a blind man, methinks thou now couldst go straightway unto my home.

SERGEANT S. Aye, I do agree with thee. Thy name now, lass, and then thou art permitted to leave.

ROSE. My name is Rose. My mother is Widow Marbury. My father was killed in battle.

SERGEANT S. To what branch of the army did he belong?

ROSE. To the Lancers, sir.

SERGEANT S. Well, I knew thy father. I knew him to be as brave a soldier as ever drew a sword, or bled in the cause of nations. Out of respect to his name and valor, I not only allow thee to retire, but furnish thee with an escort to guard thee against accident.— Here, Steinmetz, see this young girl safely domiciled, and report to me at the castle. Hurry on, now, my child, yet remember this—that ye must hold thyself in readiness to instantly obey the summons of the Prime Minister to appear before the Margrave if such is considered necessary.

Steinmetz, who has taken his station beside Rose, now leads her off C. behind Cathedral, she looking sorrowfully back at Philip and Julien as she accompanies the soldiers reluctantly.

SERGEANT S. Fall in ; look well to the prisoners, lads.

Soldiers now arrange themselves in two ranks facing the audience, with Julien and Philip in the centre—Julien in front rank and Philip in the rear rank. All promptly executing each command given by the Sergeant.

SERGEANT S. Attention- Squad, left dress—front. (Straightens front line with sword.) About, face! right wheel--forward—march !

All proceed in the direction of the O. P. side.

SERGEANT S. Halt ! Left face—forward—

Enter C. from behind Cathedral Prince Herman on horseback.

PRINCE H. (Peering at Julien) Aha! So thou art caught. By St. Michael, but this is glorious! (To Sergeant.) Officer, bind the gentleman of the sword and cloak, and deliver him up to me, and thee and thy followers shall be richly rewarded.

SERGEANT S. Rewarded? Bribed, ye mean. No, sir, I cannot comply with thy request, and furthermore, if ye make it again I'll consign thee to the loving care of the jailor of Carlsruhe. Man, thou dost forget thyself; thou art in Baden. Our laws are most severe on bribery. The people of this State—above all the noble German race—are noted for their integrity, therefore, if there were no laws against so base an act, methinks thou'd find few who'd so stain themselves as to accept a bribe. Stand aside!

PRINCE H. How darest thou address me in this manner! Thou a common soldier!

SERGEANT S. Sir Cavalier, I'm not a common soldier, I am a sergeant—a sergeant in the Margrave's reserves. Yet were I a private I'd allow no man to prefix me with common. Oh, how I hate that word, common.

PRINCE H. Well, if thou art not a common soldier—or as you phrase it—a private, thou art, at any rate, a common man, and a most insolent one.

SERGEANT S. Thou art an inflated bundle of airs and ribbons. Though belted and spurred, thou art of less consideration than the equine upon whose back thou now dost sit. Fool, bear this in mind, they alone are common whose acts are common—whose deeds are low. 'Tis such as thee, coroneted curs, who bark and snap at their betters, who stand in the way of progress, enterprise and worth. Thou art a hater and a hedger-in of freedom. The world owes thee nothing but tears, and human nature a grudge. I understand thee. Thou art an arrogant noble, conceited 'cause of thy title, imagining it makes thee of superior clay; vain courtier Mankind (a class which such as thee belong not to) may be likened unto diamonds; some are rough, some are polished, some are more beautiful than others. But he who made them knows which is the most precious gem; gaudy tinsel and highsounding degrees may dazzle the surface thinker, may obtain mouth honor, yet in themselves they are worthless, for they cannot live without merit, but merit can live without them. Taken in the proper sense, a *man* is *always* a *prince*, yet a *prince* is not *always* a *man*. Now, sir, if thou art anxious to keep thy bones in a sound condition thou'lt do as I have already commanded thee; stand aside,

PRINCE H. (After wheeling horse R.) For the present I yield to thee, my inferior. (Aside.) I believe this fellow would arrest the Margrave if he thought he was doing his duty by so performing,

SERGEANT S. Attention—squad, forward—march!

Exit sergeant, soldiers, Philip and Julien C. behind Cathedral. Music.

PRINCE H. (Anxiously.) It will never do for this stranger to escape me. No, no; not with those secrets of mine. I think the best thing to do is to get to the castle before the sergeant and his troops arrive. I will then have some chance of discovering him. May the devil and all his imps help me to succeed, say I.

Exit Prince Herman C behind Cathedral.

FOURTH SCENE.

Scene—A front perspective view, a convent in background yet boldly visible in the shadow of which nestles cottages, River Rhine, mountains cataracts, etc., in the distance. Enter Myriam Isaacs R vailed and with dagger drawn.

MYRIAM. (Throwing aside vail.) Poor Florence, I hope she's now enjoying that sweet peace which is the property of hearts united, and that little Ida, too, is perched upon her father's knee full to the lips of childish merriment. What a happy picture—what a scene for a poet's pen—for artist's brush. (Sighs.) Oh, how my temples throb—throb with that quick pace which is born of a troubled brain—a mind sorely afflicted. Heavens how I once loved that Christian knight Valdmeyer, adored him. Now, I loath him; strange that the strongest love when it changes always turns to the deepest hate. He was beautiful, and—but what is beauty without a soul, without principle; I marvel why so fair a tree should yield such vile—such bitter fruit. Why is it that man will perjure himself to afford a banquet to unhallowed passions, knowing the misery with which he must afflict the heart of her who, trusting in the truthfulness of his loving words, his affection, lays her heart—her honor, at his feet, and lives but for his pleasure. Why is it that the serpent hath influence to charm that it may but sting. Great God! what am I, a human wreck? What to-night am I here for, is it a deed of mercy? No! 'tis to kill—to murder. (Shud-

ders.) How that word chills me; murder. No, no,
'tis not to murder 'tis to avenge—to be avenged.
That's why I here do lurk--that's why I come thus
armed. I am an outcast. Who made me so but this
pretender to manhood? If he had a right to destroy
my life then I have a right to destroy his! Nor break
I with either law or equity in dealing back the blow he
gave. (Examines dagger and feels its edge.) 'Tis keen
aye, very keen Strange it seems now to be covered
o'er with moths, and each moth hath a tongue, and each
particular tongue informs me 'tis eager to slack its thirst
in blood. It must be nigh unto the time my informant
said this way the knight would come

Bell of convent strikes the first hour of morn. The watch of the convent
invisibly chant as the stroke dies away. Orchestra softly accompanying. Myriam listens attentively until quiet reigns again.

CONVENT WATCH.   As another hour of life's been
    granted,
We praise Jehovah, Omniscient—high,
In the name of the Virgin and Holy Ghost
We chant our praises to the sacred sky,
We pray, Great Father, spare us all,
Though we are ready when ere ye call,
Through blessed Jesus who dwells above
Guide us aright thou God of Love,

MYRIAM.   Thank Heaven the monks have ceased.
I am not in a mood to list unto, nor profit by the an-
thems of those holy gentiles. [Suddenly.] What if I have
strayed, it behooves me to consult my diagram lest I
tarry here for naught. (Examines a paper.) Gramarcy!
'Tis welll looked; it's not this road which runs so far behind the Monastery, but the one that passes the main
entrance. Would it were this one: not that I fear; no,
no; but this is less liable to interruption. 'Tis secluded,
therefore the fitest place. (Replaces paper.) Well, I'll
hie me to the spot, and to kill the ennui of waiting I'll
watch the silvery moon, and numerate the stars that
stud the welkin.

Exit Myriam R. re-vailing.

FIFTH SCENE.

Scene.—A front view, perspective, convent R. facade and gable standing
boldly out. A large cross with projecting rock at base L.; turrets of a castle
visible through a forest in the background. Enter R. Captain Sir Emil Valdmeyer and Lieutenant Sir Albert Josephthal, arm-in-arm; Sir Emil limps and
wears his left arm in a sling.

SIR ALBERT JOSEPHTHAL. Captain, how didst
thou injure so thyself? (Looks about.) Good, here is
a seat (assisting Valdmeyer to cross and seats him). Sit
thee on this stone a while. A little rest and the pain
will have fled thee,

SIR EMIL VALDMEYER. Damn it, Lieutenant, let
thy tongue speak sense! hast thou eyes! Why man,
if I'd sit here 'till old Cadwallader the abbot who resides
yonder, had counted each and every bead a score of
times, these hurts instead of better would be worse.

SIR ALBERT. (Shaking finger.) Ah, Captain,
Captain, I'm afraid it's a horn too much thou hast been
imbibing, got in a row, was unkindly treated. Come,
now, speak I not the truth.

SIR EMIL. If lies be truths, then thou the truth
hath spoken. It happened thus: I suppose thou art
aware that I now visit clandestinely, Eloise Lockhart,
the beautiful peasant girl who lives about a mile from
here on the borders of the Rhine. Her bewitching cottage, like herself, is a model of perfection. Lieutenant, a few more visits, backed by pretty jewels and finery, and this Juno's mine. Josephthal, women will
sell their souls for gewgaws, I'll wager a hundred rix-
dollars she'll yield to me on my next visit. Its singular
that she resembles Myriam Isaacs so closely.

SIR ALBERT. (Coldly.) Not half so singular—

SIR EMIL.—Ah, yes, I see. Not half so singular
as my crooked way of telling a story. Well, the way I
came to injure myself was—

SIR ALBERT. I care not how the injury came upon thee. Judging from the language that hath just
passed thy lips, 'twould have been a blessing if thou
hadst killed thyself instead of spraining thy ankle and
bruising an arm. I always discredited the statement as
to thy wronging Myriam, (the Jewess,) but by the
heaven above me I believe it now.

SIR EMIL. I wronged her? hell and furies, man,
she wronged herself. I was inclined to deal kindly
with the wench. I offered to relieve her of her burden,
our child, you understand; I also offered her a goodly
sum of money. All these kindnesses she refused, saying I must either wed her or die. Well, to keep her
still I went through a sort of mock wedding, and when
the fool found out the cheat she committed suicide.

This is all from Alpha to Omega. (Aside.) All that he shall know. (Aloud) Thou canst see plainly I was quite tender with her, the saucy minx.

SIR ALBERT. (Fiercely.) Tender! Sir, 'twas like the tenderness of the Vulture when he loosens his talons to take a firmer hold. Had I known thee as I do now I would have plucked out both mine eyes before I'd joined the troops which thou, in being its commander doth but disgrace. I knew thee to be a cold and callous man, yet I little dreamed thou wert so base,—so hardened a scoundrel. Say what thou wilt I believe thou hast dealt foully with poor Myriam, and in the name of my dear departed mother (bares his head,, I swear I'll rest me not 'till I have unmasked thy villainy. From this hour I am the champion of little Eloise, and woe unto thee if harm befalls her through any act of thine. Furthermore, I'll instantly petition to be transferred to another command, and if my petition be not immediately granted I shall resign, for I should feel a stain upon my escutcheon—mine honor lost, if I longer consorted with one so contemptible. Oh, Heaven! why dost thou let the evil prosper so? There are men—aye, and I am one of them—who've been all their lives sighing—thirsting for the love—the affection of a true heart, and yet never possessed themselves of this joy Like some "Ignus-fatuus," it has always eluded them whilst yon knave hath had it thrust upon him, and set not so much store by it as I would a simple rose that had once adorned the fragrant bosom of a lovely woman. Sir, I go, yet I shall remember to send a servant to thee with thy horse. Captain from this time forth we are enemies.

Exit R. Sir Albert, Sir Emil, looking quizzically after him.

SIR EMIL. I see through this, yea, as clearly as through a crystal drop of water. My good Lieutenant's jealous, he loves Eloise—he takes this as a fitting opportunity to cut with me ; well, so be it, its nothing new ; the men were always jealous of me. Why ? because I could take their sweethearts from them. Women are light, giddy ; yet I love the fair creatures, that is, I desire them ; I suppose that's love. That fool of a Lieutenant was not astray as regards my taking here a little rest, for by the beard of Mohomet's goat I do feel better· I think unto my house I now could walk without assistance· Yet I suppose I'd better remain

here until my servant comes. (Yawns.) I wonder
whether Myriam's really under the sod ? Pshaw ! she
must be ; to have escaped the dogs I set upon her track
was impossible. I held the villains firmly in my power,
they dared not betray me, besides, the price I set upon
her death was enough to have tempted better me than
they to the execution of such a deed. Bah ! the worms
have held their banquet o'er her this many a day. Yet
I do believe that if spirits—

*At this juncture, Myriam, with face vailed, who has stealthily entered L.
and gain the side of Sir Emil, prepares to strike. Her presence being detected
she quickly conceals her weapon behind her.*

SIR EMIL. (Starting.) In the name of all the
gods at once, who art thou ?

MYRIAM· Does not thy conscience tell thee ?

SIR EMIL. I have no conscience ; I have not
room within my breast for such a fool.

MYRIAM. The coward color which from thy face
hath fled, belies what thou dost say. Thou hast a conscience ; 'tis that which pricks thee now. Ye may sti-
fle her for a time, but as sure as there's a future, she
will raise up and put thee down. Aha ! ye tremble—
her grip's upon thee.

SIR EMIL. [Recovering himself.] What mean
ye here at this weird hour, so closely muffled in dismal
black so thickly vailed. If thou art the devil's mother,
speak, for Emil Valdmeyer knows not even the meaning of fear. If all the Hydra-headed monsters that
swim the deep, or crawl on land, were here to do me
battle I would not blanch.

MYRIAM, Bravado—the stale old trick that pol-
troons summon to their aid to cloak the craven that
dwells within their hearts. [Aside] I must get him
off his guard. [Aloud.] Thou wouldst know me ?
Well, answer me this riddle and thou'll half discover
me. What is that which the Almighty hath not seen,
nor ever can see, yet every human being may behold !

SIR EMIL. [Mockingly.] Now, my Lady Hob-
goblin, if thou hast armed thyself with conundrums
freshly filched from forgotten dream-books, and mean-
dered here with intent base—aye, mind made up to
spring, as it were, 'pon some unsuspecting traveller and
propound a riddle, let me tell thee I'm the very worst
man thou couldst have waylaid. For I'm thicker than

a fog in catching a riddle's point. Besides, to be plain
with thee, I think thy riddle's a sorry one. Why, ha !
ha, ha,—pshaw, Mrs. Ghost, I—

MYRIAM.   Stop thou deuse witted babbler, I will
both repeat the question and render thee the answer.
What is that which the Almighty hath not seen, nor
ever can see, yet every human being may behold ? His
equal.

SIR EMIL..   Mrs. Ghost, thou art a whole book of
puzzles. Thy conundrum's a very deep one, still I'm
disappointed.   •

MYRIAM.   Why so facetious, gentleman ?

SIR EMIL.   Because I find thee only an equal, after thou hast worked my imagination up to believe thee
something more. This is hardly fair, Mrs. Ghost.
[Leans forward laughing immoderately.]

MYRIAM.   Knave, I am yet but half discovered.
Know I'm also thy death [stabs Sir Emil twice then un-
vails], thou matchless tool of sin.   Charon's boat doth
now await thee.   At last we are quits.

As soon as Myriam stabs Sir Emil he starts up and places his hand to his
side, staggering C.   Then he turns and stares wildly at her.

SIR EMIL.   By the Archangel Michael, the grave
has either given up its dead, tombs refused to perform
the office of sepulchres, and spectres walk abroad, or
else thou art Myriam Isaacs.

MYRIAM.   Yes. I am Myriam Isaacs—Myriam the
Jewess, whose home ye destroyed, whose happiness ye
blasted, whose chastity, through, deceit, ye stole.   I
am here to keep my word.

SIR EMIL.   Curse thee and thy riddle, for through
it thou hast riddled me.   Had I not taken thee latter-
ly for a rustic, dwelling hard by, bent upon a lark
at ghostly business, thou wouldst not thus have
triumphed.   Hadst thou been content with the terms I
once offered thee—which, on the whole were very liber-
al--accepted the money, gone about thy business, and
left me to myself, all would have run smoothly on.   But
ye forced me to marry thee.   [Aside.]   What am I
saying? [Aloud.]   I mean thou didst so strive to do.
This brought on thee the avalanche which hath wrecked
thy life, and robbed it of its joys.

MYRIAM.   [Excitedly.]   I wanted to force thee to
marry me. Fiend, didst thou not promise me so to do ?

After winning my heart, after (through mine innocence and the love I bore thee,)thou had stmade me but a toy to thee. Why,man, we were scarce acquainted ere thou proffered marriage. Hast thou forgotten the nigh:—here,on the outskirts of Carlsruhe, in the shadow of this very convent, when, with arm around my waist,ye said: " Myriam, I want thee for a wife," swearing to be true by yonder cross, the emblem of thy faith—I mean the Christian faith—for thou art faithless in all respects.

SIR EMIL.   lAside.] By the rod of old King Moses, but the tigress is aroused. She'll consummate her threat if help arrives not shortly. I must prolong the argument.   These crippled limbs, and the gashes she hath made on my poor side, puts me ' hors de combat,'* (Aloud).   What couldst thou have expected were not I a nobleman,and thou but the child of peasants,—worse than all a Jewess—though I'll admit your family were respectable.   But what of that? What signifies the respectability of peasants. Foolishly conceited must thou have been to have imagined that a noble would stoop so low as to mate with a peasant's daughter.

MYRIAM.   Peace miscreant ; my father though a peasant was yet thy better. He was good and true, and such are beyond thy comprehension.   There have been those born of poverty, who've risen to princely dignities, whose hands have the rod of Empire swayed ; whose occupancy of the Chair of State was attended with all the splendor and greatness that waits on Genius, and the glory of whose deeds are more imperishable than the monuments raised to commemorate their acts; whose nobility was of nature's loftiest type, emanating from him whose potency to place,out-ranked all earthly station. But thy nobility—thy kind of nobility (if the word may be so slandered) consists but in a piece of parchment and the seal of Government, more oft procured by treachery, robbery, or sycophancy, than by honest merit. Such as ye are strangers to all save vice, and the humblest mortal that walks in rectitude towers o'er thee as does the sturdy oak above the toadstool's cankered stalk, as to the Jew ye fling at me.   Remember, that he of Nazareth who Israelites as well as Christians respect, was of Hebrew blood—a Jew.

---

* Not in a condition to fight.

Man's raised not 'bove his fellow man
By birth, or creed, or country ;
'Tis worth, heart, and loyalty to tru·h
Wherein distinction lies.

SIR EMIL. Myriam, thou hast grown in eloquence.

MYRIAM. Emil Valdmeyer ; thou hast grown in villainy, Sir: flattery will avail thee as little as sneers ! I have come to be avenged Nothing short of thy miserable existence will satisfy me. (Aside.) Would that I had finished him in the first stroke ; yet after the loss of so much blood he cannot hold on, against me—besides he's badly bruised.

(Myriam rushes forward, Sir Emil grapples with her, they wrestle about the stage.)

SIR EMIL. (Wildly.) What ho ! Cadwallader, come forth ! Come out ye shaven crowns ! I'm being murdered ! Come forth I say ! What ho within ! What ho ! What —·

[At this juncture, Myriam again stabs Sir Emil, who then falls, after which he rips open his coat at the breast and produces a paper which he essays to destroy, but dies before accomplishing it. Myriam picks up paper and reads it excitedly.

MYRIAM. Do I dream—no ; here is the proof, the veritable tangible proof—the evidence now in my hand, I see it all ! he was himself cheated, but on discovery hath either stolen or bribed the person who held this bond, this marriage contract ; to put him in possession of it. He must but recently have obtained the document, or else it long ere this had been in flames. Perhaps this arm in sling has something to do with this certificate, for he would hazard life or limb to carry out a scheme, for good or evil. (Drops dagger, and stretches both hands prayerfully up, yet clings firmly to paper.) I am not then a dishonest thing, thank Heaven, thank Heaven.

Myriam now falls, fainting yet firmly clings to paper with left hand. Enter at this junction L. Abbot Cadwallader and some monks.

ABBOT CADWALLADER. Thou art right good Brother Andrew—thou art right.

BROTHER ANDREW. Sir Abbot, before the will of Heaven clothed me in Priestly habilaments, 'Squire was I to the Margrave's brother; father of the Princess Louisa ye know, Prince Cederick, Duke of Carlsruhe was as valiant a Knight as ever couched a lance, or drew a blade. 'Twas with this noble gentleman I gain-

ed my scars and the knowledge of the art of war.   The
braying trump the battle's din, the clash of arms are still
within mine ears—groans, shouts the yell of the
victor, and the curse of the vanquished.   Good Abbot
I can smell out an encounter or battle, or anything
that smacks of war at almost any distance ; so when I
caught that yell which it appears none else of the
Brotherhood seemed to hear, I urged the quickening of
our pace, because I was convinced that blood was being spilt in close proximity to us.   An old soldier ne'er
mistakes the sound of strife, whether the number engaged be few or many.

MYRIAM.   (Raising on one knee.)   Thou knowest
full well a slave am I to kindness, yet wear I about me
that which makes the brooking of an injury as impossible as the changing of the earth its orbit.   (Arises to
her feet looks wildly about.)   I have kept my word ; I
said I would, I said I —

[Myriam now staggers, and is about to fall, but is prevented by Brother
Andrew.]

BRO. A.   Daughter, cheer up, thou art with
friends. (Looks into Myriam's face then turns to Abbot.)
Most worthy Abbot, if I mistake not, this woman is of
Hebrew extraction.

ABBOT.   (After gazing at Myriam.)   Yes, she is
an Israelite.   I fear the extravagance of her beauty
hath brought about this bloody picture ; I'm almost
certain it's the old tale, a deceived woman avenging
herself on her treacherous lover.   Well, it matters not
to us what be her faith, she's at least one of God's creatures.   The laws of our Holy Church are the laws of
Heaven, and the laws of Heaven are merciful, "Do ye
unto others as ye have would others do unto thee."   So
said the Master.

ALL.   Aye, good Abbot, aye.

Enter R. at this juncture a Grand Justice with attendants, all armed.

GRAND JUDGE.   Wherefore all this chattering ;
this polyglot confusion (if not of Babel) of shaven
crowns.   (Spying Sir Emil's body.)   Aha ! a dead
man !   Who did this work ?   Come—render quickly to
me an answer.

ABBOT.   As to this blood letting, I know no more
than does thyself ; but who art thou that puts questions
with such a show of high authority ; if I did not know

who was guardian of the throne, I should say ye held Vallenstein's place being therefore Chancellor.

GRAND JUD. Though not Prime Minister, my power is scarcelly less great. I am Alonzo Del Fernandez (the exile Prince), now Grand Judge of Baden. In other words, I am the law in corporal form. Now sir, who art thou that dares to question the law.

ABBOT. My Lord, we are as thy worship can plainly see ; Holy Monks, yon Sacred Convent is where we abide, we are members of the powerful order of the Holy Cross o'er this branch of the fraternity the dignified rank of Abbot do I hold. I am Cadwallader the Abbot. In Brother Andrew here thou dost behold our Honorable Secretary—in other words we are the Church in corporal form. Dare ye question the Church.

GRAND JUD. I dare when the Church grows insolent and forgets its place.

ABBOT. When the law plays tyrant, and runs not its proper groove, so dare I.

BRO. A. So thou art the ex-Duke of Granada ; or as ye put it, Alonzo Del Fernandez, the Exile Prince. I have heard much of thee, though never before did I set eyes upon thy substance. Would to God thy Spanish brothers had strung thee up in gibbet, then thou hadst never disturbed our sacred faith in this quarter. For that ye hate our ancient religion thy decrees make it manifest, and though thou hast held office here but six short months, thou hast done us much harm. Curse on thy misleading speeches to the people—maledictions on thy interfering restrictions.

GRAND JUD. Go too, thou peculating son of psalms.

BRO. A. The compliment we return thou legalized pilferer, ye of the law bear close resemblance to a pair of shears, which never cut themselves but that between. Some three and twenty days ago, I had audience with the Margrave. After leaving his royal presence, I strode down the lofty stoop of the Palace and stood meditating in the shadow of that splendid pile. I was aroused from my reverie by two sentinels. Saith the first, " See, there comes Abraham Levi." The second replied, " it was no strange sight to behold this percentage-moth roving 'bout the executive mansion; that he was a vulture whose prey was cabinet ministers." " Right well

I know all this," saith the first, " yet as he is now, 'tis most uncommon and wonderful; for dost thou not observe he has his hands in his own pockets ? At this, both sentries laughed, and resumed their measured tread, whilst Levi passed from view into the spacious hall, I leaned me against the base of a massive column, and mused. Sir Judge, can your highness divine what then I thought?

GRAND JUD. I cannot, neither do I care to know.

BRO. A. (Bows.) Nevertheless, as breath is but the air, and air is free, I feel at liberty to tell thee uninvited, 'twas this—I thought what a loss it was to the knights of law that Sir Abraham was not counted among its members. What a splendid judge would he not make. How readily would he stain the ermine black, as too often the wearers of it do.

GRAND JUD. Hold, churlish monk—'twas ever thus—church with justice—militant. The reason her motto doth contain, which reads, rule or ruin. Ye may hurl invective s at the ermine, yet with far more certitude can I affirm that the ample folds of priestly vestments do as often conceal the depraved as the venerable. When first I entered this scene, I took ye for disguised robbers, and I was right, for who thieves more secretly than the church. First it steals conscience, then liberty, and ends by taking the purse. I scorn it. It's a stupendous subterfuge Its bulwark is the fears of the ignorant and the credulous. It says be meek, thirst not for fame, yet is itself most ambitious and arrogant, delighting in mummery and foolish display. It says to its chanted followers, trust in God, while it alone trusts in the bloody sword and death-dealing cannon. It says, give up thy gold,—'tis trash, mere stuff. the root of all evil, yet is always ready to take this root whene'er it comes within its reach. Gold is its God. I believe in Heaven and a pure religion. But this is not religion, 'tis a money-making business.

BRO. A. I'll stand no more, thou accursed infidel.

Brother Andrew now rushes forward, and raises his staff to strike. The Judge draws his sword. The Abbot catches Myriam in his arms, and commands Brother Andrew to desist.

ABBOT. (Waving his staff). Hold, good Andrew. Brothers, stay him, hold him firmly.

Monks seize the Secretary, and bring him back to his former place beside the Abbot.

BRO. A.   Most noble Cadwallader, why did your worship stop mine hand? Has he not grown impious.

ABBOT.   Yea, honored brother, but the church teaches not with blows. The ministry of God gives its lessons through love ; 'tis our province to return good for evil, thus shaming the base from their sinful ways, so taught the Master, and we will prove recreant to our high mission if otherwise we act. Yet I do forgive thy haste for the soldier in the: e'en I myself was sorely tried by him, and did somewhat stray in speech from our holy office, which should be as it ever has been — one of mildness and love. (Turning to the Judge.) My son, retrace thy misguided steps, ere it be too late, (With dignity.) The Church is sacred—the Church is truth ; to affront the Church is to offer insolence to Heaven, a sin, most deadly, and calls for punishment most bitter.

GRAND JUD.   To my thinking ther's little analogy between Heaven and the Church. I leave thee, but in the name of the Margrave and the law I hold thee all responsible for the safety of this body, and that woman, too. For, in my mind, a party to this work I think she be.

ABBOT.   With the laws of Baden have we good knowledge. This fair creature shall be held in gentle custody. This body shall to our convent be conveyed, and treated there with all the respect due it as the tabernacle where once abided an immortal soul When the noble coroner desires to hold his sitting his Lordship hath but his pleasure to acquaint us with, till then we claim authority.

GRAND JUD.   If I were as stern and arrogant as ye say, I would arrest each and every person now within the sound of my voice that go to make up thy party instead of trusting to thy word for the reproduction of this woman and her victim, I am empowered by law so to do. Yet for the testing of thy priestly honor, I'll this time forego the privilege. But, Sir Abbot, if thou dost attempt any double dealing, woe betide thee.

Exit R. Grand Judge and attendants ; bell in the convent strikes the second hour of morn ; The abbot and monks bow their heads ; The convent watch chant accompanied by the orchestra.

CONVENT WATCH,   Another hour of lies been granted,

We praise Jehovah, Omniscient—high,
In the name of the Virgin and the Holy Ghost,
We chant our praises to the sacred sky,
We pray great Father spare us all,
Though we are ready when ee'r ye call
Through blessed Jesus who dwells above,
Guide us aright thou God of love.

ABBOT. Let one of you good brothers haste within the monastery and toll the funeral bell, that all may know that death is in our midst.

Exit into convent a monk who immediately tolls bell ; Brother Andrew secures Myriam's dagger as monk leaves.

ABBOT. Some of you look after the dead, then follow close upon our heels. Come, good Andrew ; come, poor maid.

Some monks now take hold of Sir Emil's body and follow the Abbot and Bro. Andrew, who together support Myriam. The rest follow the body. The entire party look sorrowful and downcast. All exit into convent. Bell tolls until every one has disappeared within monastery. Solemn music.

THIRD SCENE.

Scene.—The ame as first scene in first act, Gottlieb and Catherine seated Gottlieb as before, and Catherine on his left. Lamp burning on table. Florence Stover with her little daughter Ida clinging closely to her stands C. Florence is weeping. Her husband Leopold (who half faces Gottlieb) leans moodily against mantle piece, all discovered.

CATHERINE. [To Leopold.] Another year with all its hopes to life hath been born, show thy thanks therefore to the Creator by forgiveness of your wife. Her heart beats but for thee—'tis throbbing for thee now. Have pity, if only for thy child.

LEOPOLD STOVER. For the child's sake much will I do, as perhaps mine may she be, the doubts, benefit I'll give her to please thee and good friend Gottlieb. Even Florence for naught shall want under the circumstances I cannot find it proper more to yield.

FLORENCE. Leopold—Leopold, tell me what to do, thy wrath to appease. gladly would I lay me in the grave if in the eternal sleep thy forgiving kiss with me wert buried. Doubt not that thou art the father of this child, for in the name of all the saints I swear ye be, was not she three round months in age afore I fled thee. Did not her entry into this world under thine own roof take place.

LEOPOLD. Yes, thou sayest truly as to her being born under my roof. Yet for all that, how knowest I,

that I in fact her father be. Lydia Breiftzen said on oath
at stated periods, when my back was squarely turned,
that Parson Von Beecherton was a welcome visitor.
He never, (when I were at home) thought of paying his
respects to me.   In fact not on the best of terms were
we, yet it be not strange for the husband to be distaste-
full, when the wife is desired, and love the wife when
encouragement we receive.   Now, as it was with him
ye fled how can I help it doubt my being the father to
thy child.   For in thy flight alone thou didst herald
thy prostitution, and couple thy daughter's name with
bastardy.

FLORENCE.   I did not flee with Parson Von Beecherton, as oft in my letters, (not one of which ye deigned
to answer,) I informed thee a thousand times and which
thy language I'm convinced ye never even read.

LEOPOLD.   Letters?   In all thy absence not so
much as one poor line did I receive.

FLORENCE   Then ye know not of Lydia's treachery.

LEOPOLD.   Lydia's treachery?   What enigma is
this?

FLORENCE.   Is it possible thou hast not e'en so
much as a suspicion.   (Aside.)   Ah, Myriam, perhaps
spoke the truth.   A reunion may be close at hand.
Oh, how my soul swells within me—stirred up by this
fond hope. [Aloud.] Husband. mark well what now
I say.   The Parson admired me, 'tis true yet I fled thy
house through no design of his.   Lydia loved thee—
and finding in me a barrier to her bliss hated me, scheming night and day 'till our separation she produced.
But the power of powers had his eye upon her, and his
vengeance speedily followed.   For as ye remember, she
sickened and died—died whilst thou were attending business in Radstadt.   Being convinced thy face
she'd never again behold, and not wishing to put her
cruel act on paper, she made her sailor brother, then
bound for sea, promise to tell thee, at the earliest opportunity, all the mischief she had done unto our homes.
At Milan her brother, in a duel was killed ; Brother
Andrew, now secretary of the convent over which the
Abbot Cadwallader presides, was the priest who attended him, and to whom he told the story of my wrongs.
Her brother said he left the records of his sisters crime

in trusty hands, and that thou must certainly, soon after he sailed, have discovered all. I'll warrant that Brother Andrew will gladly testify to all I now have said. I fled thee because I loved thee ; I thought I stood in the way of thy happiness ; I thought thou hadst transferred thy heart to Lydia, and wouldst rejoice to have me far away. But, oh ! my husband ! thou canst never know the pain it cost me in leaving thy dear side.

LEOPOLD. All this to me is news. But I believe thee. Wouldst that I had been clearer sighted and less credulous.

FLORENCE. Would we both had, my husband !

LEOPOLD. I could now thy flight forgive if, in thine absence thou hadst remained true. For thou canst not deny, though we credit thee with not eloping with the Parson, that thou didst not harken to his pleadings, nor yield thyself to his wishes. Oh, Florence, there's the sting, for when I think of thee, passive in his arms, he feeding on thy young beauty, drinking up thy love, which Heaven had willed alone sacred unto me, I grow mad— mad !

FLORENCE. No defense do I make of my unhallowed conduct with this man whose tongue in deceit was schooled, made insidious by the oil of hypocrisy. But this I'll say—when I left thee I was in that state of flexibility which may be likened unto wax, readily shaping itself to the moulder's forms, and, as I thought thy love for me was buried, or rather bestowed upon another, I scarce knew or cared what I did. I had but one wish, and that was to render myself oblivious to the past· Leopold, tell me truly didst thou remain proof against fair Lydia's charms when ye presumed my heart had ceased to beat in unison with thine.

LEOPOLD. I should not, were this an ordinary affair, feel it my duty to respond to such a question. 'Twould be most ungallant to reveal a woman's sin, especially when to the tattler she gave her honor's keeping. But as this wretched girl hath forfeited her right, I will reply. 'Tis natural when the heart is full, ye turn to those who seem to pity thee—who bear about thy grief as though it were their own. So did this Lydia-- I mean she did so appear to do. But to abridge an unhappy tale let this suffice ; I learned to admire her greatly ; she was my--my mistress.

FLORENCE.   Husband, when I discovered how
things stood, how we both had been cheated, I nearly
lost my reason.   I drove the base gownsman from me
as though he were some poisonous reptile whose touch
was annihilation, (drawing herself up grandly) and from
that hour I have been a mother and a wife.

*Florence now leads Ida to Leopold, both kneel before him. Leopold
weeps and turns away his head.*

GOTTLIEB.   Leopold, I am an old man.   The book
of time hath marked me on its debit side with nigh unto eighty years.   My good Catherine there hath turned
three-score, whilst thou art but in the middle tide of
life, thy lovely mate yet in her youth.   Human joys like
our existence is of short duration.   Throw not the cup
of happiness aside whilst ye may grasp it.   Think me
no meddler ; I only speak out of an honest friendship I
hold for both.

*Leopold turns, stretches out his arms.   Florence and Ida arise and rush for-
ward, they embrace.   Gottlieb and Catherine look at each other joyfully.*

FLORENCE.   Again, I have a husban l, my own,
my dear—dear Leopold.

IDA.   An her has a pappa, a dear—dear pappa.

LEOPOLD.   Ebon-visaged night, now gives place
to bright faced day.   Again the sky is clear—serenely
clear.   (Kisses Florence and Ida fondly)   A new
path—a broad road—a great highway, stretches out before me, and once more my heart swells with all its
pristine hopes.

GOTTLIEB.   (Placing cane on table.)   With all
my soul I say, Amen !   (Stretching forth his hands.)
Hallowed Father—dispenser of all good—ye before
whom human wisdom is but as foolishness—I thank thee
for the happy termination of this crushing sorrow
which hath so long cast its blight upon a home, and
kept asunder two living hearts.   May it be thy will
that so long as they do here abide, that they 'll be visit-
ed with all the joys that mankind's heir to.   (Turns to
Leopold, Florence and Ida, who stand with heads
bowed respectfully throughout the thanksgiving.)   Bless
thee, my children—bless thee.   This is one of the hap-
piest moments of my life·   Forsooth I fear too much
pleasure to dwell long with old Gottlieb.

*Leopold and Florence with Ida, now cross to settee and seat themselves,
Ida on Leopold's knee.   Florence holds his hand.   They talk in dumb show and
fondle little Ida.   At this juncture some one knocks at the door.*

GOTTLIEB.—Wife, I think our Philip's returned. (Glances at clock.) By St· John, who'd believe it ; see for thyself, Catherine—three o'clock.

CATHERINE. (Looking at clock.) I wonder not this night, at time's fleet pace. For the curtain hath but fallen on a drama most real, with scenes so vivid that one forgets all else in watching them. But why our Philip tarries out so long I cannot conjecture. I fear me something has happened the boy.

Knocking is now heard louder.

GOTTLIEB. Yes, wife, our Philips's at the door, dost thou not hear him ? Ha–ha ! Rose hath caught it this night.

Catherine opens door. Enter some of the Margrave's guard followed by Captain Sir Albert Josephthal. Catherine rushes to Gottlieb who seizes his cane and stands erect. Leopold, Florence and Ida start up from the settee in amazement. Suddenly as if just recognizing Sir Albert, they all bow and change their defiant looks to smiles.

GOTTLIEB. Thou art welcome to our house, Sir Albert, But why this armed visit ?

SIR ALBERT. Good Master Montagna, a painful duty have I to perform. Thou and thy worthy wife must I arrest, so reads the Royal order ; surely it's some mistake, must be, and will speedily be set aright. Yet doth it hurt me all the same to offer so much as even the shadow of an insult to so valiant a soldier as old Sergeant Montagna. But be not alarmed. The Margrave's as noble as he's wise.

GOTTLIEB, Thanks, Lieutenant Your honor, I'm not worth so much respect. 'Tis surely as thou sayest, a mistake. Yet will we go peaceably with thee.

CATHERINE. (Aside.) My poor, dear son——my darling boy, This will sorely afflict thee. Thy morrow's banquet will no doubt be a feast of sighs.

SIR ALBERT. Brave Montagna, I am no longer a Lieutenant of Artillery. I'm now a Captain—not only a captain, but a Captain commander over the personal guards of His Liege the Margrave. I saved him from being, perhaps mortally, wounded by an infuriated courtier whose arrest he had commanded ; cause robbing the Treasury, and for the act was created chief of the body-guard of His soverign Excellence. There being a vacancy through the death of Captain Lutzberg, The Margrave hath taken a strong fancy to me, as much on account of a petition I placed within his hands as the saving of his life. He treats me so kindly, and speaks so highly about me. that I fear he will spoil me.

CATHERINE.   Captain, thou hast always stood well favored in our eyes. Thou art a gentleman, sir, and hath too much of sense to be easily set wrong.

LEOPOLD.   A true soldier always is a gentleman

Captain Sir Albert Josephthal bows at this juncture, as one overcome with the weight of compliment.

GOTTLIEB.   (Turning to Leopold.) Do you and your family o'er this house keep guard and break to Philip the news of our misfortune as gently as possible. (To Captain.) Sir, as soon as we are dressed befitting-ly we will accompany thee.

FOURTH ACT—FIRST SCENE.

Scene.—An antechamber in the Margrave's palace, at Carlsruhe. Enter R· Gottlieb and Catherine Montagna, Gottlieb using a cane.

GOTTLIEB.—Did I understand thee to say ye saw our Philip in the hall yonder.

CATHERINE·   Thou hast the words of my mouth repeated.

GOTTLIEB.   Let's seek him, then, for perhaps the poor boy is now there waiting, thinking to gain a word or too with us.

CATHERINE.   No, we will not seek him; that were useless. We would not find him now, Gottlieb. When first we were made prisoners my heart sank with-in me, for I imagined straight-way that Philip into harm had fallen, which by some strange circumstance both implicated thou and I.   But now I believe the ac-cident that may have befallen him will to our house a goodly blessing prove. Perhaps Philip hath committed a brave act—saved young Julien's life, done something noble—something, the which I know not, yet something that merits a high reward.

GOTTLIEB.   If this be so, what need was there in making captives of both his parents.

CATHERINE.   His Liege at first may have been mistakened, intending therefore to punish. But dis-covering now his mistake, transforms chastisement into a requital of service. As Philip and the Prince (for they were both together) passed by the hall door where then I stood, I heard Lord Julien say, " Philip hie with me to my room and don a better dress that ye may ap-

pear before the Margrave as more becomes thee. Mark
well that sentence, Gottlieb. As more becomes thee.
Surely thy mind must see by this, that Philip hath fallen heir to great profit, and we are now but gently held
to witness the honors heaped upon our son.

GOTTLIEB· This the case may be, but heads of
States do soon forget, and when they do not they sel-
dom take this fashion in the bestowal of rewards. Catherine, we are poor and poverty gets but little breadth
of notice.

CATHERINE. Tut, tut, man ! we are not beggars,
thou art a soldier—an old soldier tried and found trusty,
I and all the world with good Leopold do concur, that
a true soldier is a gentleman. Besides the land is deb-
tor to thee for much lost blood. Feel more thy worth and
that recompense is but the due of merit. Gottlieb do
not entirely lose sight of having once been well-to-do.

GOTTLIEB. On this earth 'tis not what ye were
but what ye be. A bold usurper firmly seated in our
Margrave's throne wouldst be respect by all the Princes
of Europe, and obeyed at home. He might have sprung
from mendicants and be stamped with illegitimacy, but
what of that, so long as he be sovereign, Lord Paramount o'er the land. What service would it render unto
our good Ethelbert in having the right to say, I have
been a reigning monarch. Though I am dethroned
and dare not set foot in Baden, yet am I a sovereign.
Though I am an outcast to my country—though I am
poor and oft know want, still am I a Prince. The very
knave who now durst not meet his gaze, wouldst mock at
him in such a straight. Catherine, so long as thou
canst force obedience—so long as it profits not to cross
thee, thou wilt have respect No, it is not what ye
were , but what ye be.

CATHERINE. (With dignity.) Churlish minds, I
will admit, do so consider. But, sir, a hero stands in
the foremost ranks of worth, a true man is nature's fullest joy. and he that scorns him 'cause of poverty or failure affronts the Host above us.

GOTTLIEB. I never felt that much of greatness
won I about, unless it be the great pains that have
been most zealous visitors to my wounded leg these
three years. Now, as to Philip's turning out a great
man, I should not be at all surprised. Yet patiently
will I wait, for time makes havoc with mysteries.

Enter R. Captain Sir Albert Josephthal.

SIR ALBERT.   My good old friends, ye must not
leave the waiting chamber without permission.   I shall
be forced to place about thee a guard if ye both keep
wandering so around the palace.   This is now the third
time that I have cautioned thee.   Come, follow me,
and remain, I prithee, where I place thee.   When the
Prime Minister summons thee to appear before the
Margrave thou wilt be in readiness.

GOTTLIEB.   (To Sir Albert.)   Thou shalt be obeyed.   (To Catherine.)   Attention—attention, wife (staggers a trifle).   Right dress, there, Gottlieb – right dress,
eyes front, Catherine—heads up, breasts out—

CATHERINE.   (Taking Gottlieb's arm.)   Come, sir
come ; seest thou not the Captain waiting beyond for
us ?

GOTTLIEB.   Forward—march !

Exit Gottlieb and Catherine R., Catherine leading Gottlieb by the arm.
Gottlieb endeavors to appear soldierly in his walk.

SECOND SCENE.

Scene.—Hall in the Margrave's palace.   Enter R. Pauline Sinn (a maid to
the Princess Louisa) followed by Wiseacre (the Court Jester) in full dress, carrying in his hand the sceptre proper to his office.

WISEACRE.   I be a fool, my lass, 'tis true.
Only a Prince's jester,
Yet doth mine office require,
Aye, take deeper thought
Than half the noble of this court
Have breadth of mind for.

PAULINE SINN.   Ho, ho, our jester grows tragic,
gives now blank verse by way of entertainment.   Gramercy Wiseacre, be this all in thy play ?   If so I'll have
thee read it from first to last.   It's a dead hit I suppose.

WISEA'.   Cease, malapert !   Prophets are unknown
in the histrionic art.   No dramatist can tell with certitude whether a play will succeed or not when placed
upon the theatric boards.   The public is fickle, giving
more heed unto a trashy pantomime (a mere tinseled
spectacle, devoid of sense or thought) a highly colored
improbable, and glaringly wrought melodrama– a light
and silly tragicomedy, or a nude and gaudy burlesque,
which in blank verse I'll say—

Where the ladies' dresses are cut so low
And cut so high—
That a mere drapery (looped up in plaits about
each charming waist)
Is all that covers them,
And for this kind of theatrical exposure
Bald headed sin seems to have the strongest taste.

PAULINE· Poor gentlemen, to be pitied are they
Yet on mature consideration, I think it may be said,
there's not a man who'll refuse the taking in of a lega-
cy. (Shakes herself playfully.) But, lad, I protest
against the familiar manner in which ye handle the
name of Sir—my name, sir, giving it as it were a black-
end eye.

WISEA'. The coloring is subservient to thy will,
not mine, my lass.

PAULINE. I differ with thee, sir Jester. Surely I
am most unguarded and quite helpless. For doth not
mine own cognomen conspire against me, and endeavor
to debase me. If ye doubt it look but in our family
Bible, and there you'll see it continually says, *Pauline
Sinn.*

Both laugh heartily.

WISEA'. If thou art going to fling about such wit
as this, I'll resign thee my crown, my sceptre and my
station.

PAULINE. [Pertly.] Well, whatever thou dost,
there's one thing I pray thou'll yield me not, and that's
a place within thy, poem.

WISEA'. (Vexatiously.) Suacy, lass—think ye
that with mine own hand I would—Oh, hang it. Let
this suffice. Thou art not there to mar its lofty spirit.

PAULINE. So then, thou hast another girl?

WISEA'. My girls are many, yet there's only one
I love.

PAULINE. [Putting up hands to face and feigning
to weep.] Of course that one's not me. But ye shall
repent of thy nice deception. What's to pay me for
all the huggings and kisses I've let thee have. Ah,
me alack o-day, was ever maid so treated. [Suddenly
removing hand from face and clenching them.] Aha,
but I have thee on the hip. I'll information give
unto our beautious Princess how, while once she
bathed ye peeped at her:

WISEA'. I care not if thou dost, our Royal Lady's but a woman, and, like all her sisters, inclines to adulation. I'll wager thee ten marks that if ye do inform, that in less than twice five minutes time I'll have so flattered her that mine offence will change its hue, and myself stand more favored in her eye. My virgin this is but another proof of my name's correctness. Ye see I know where to look, how to look, and what be worth the looking at (smacking lips, places hands on stomach.) She's the dream of a Turk, yet, Lena, thou hast beauty enough for me ; thy love is all I ask.

PAULINE. When a Prince's Fool doth talk of love it hath but the appearance of a jest. Yet if thou'll make me thy drama's heroine, I'll clasp hands with thee, and ye may do with me as thou wilt. What says my Wiseacre ?

WISEA'. A truce I say all thy female tricks. Be but thine own sweet self and thou art heroine enough. I dare not place thee in my poem for fear the hero'd steal thee ; I am too jealous. The fittest place I know for thee is—

PAULINE. (Peering into Wiseacre's face as she draws near to him.) Where ?

WISEA'. In these arms (embraces her) in these arms.

PAULINE. Unhand me, villain, else a guardsman will I call ! (Throws arms about Wiseacre's neck, and lays head on his shoulder.) Dost thou hear ?

WISEA'. Thy guardsman's here. (Kisses her eagerly.) See how he defends thee !

PAULINE. Nurse thy strength for vigorous is the foe.

WISEA'. In o'er a hundred battles it's ne'er been known to flag.

Both come forward C., Wiseacre R., Pauline L. Sing the following.

WISEA'.   When Hymen's knot is tied,
             And thou my bride's become
             On life's river will we glide,
             " Two hearts that beat as one."

Chorus   { Oh the hours of Wedded life
           { Are rife with pleasure,
BOTH   { And a husband or a wife
           { Are each a treasure.

PAULINE.   When the moon is at her height,
            We'll wander to the dell,
            And with souls aglow with love,
            In fond embraces dwell.

Chorus {
Вотн {   Oh, the hours of wedded life, etc., etc.

The blast of a bugle is now heard as if at no great distance. Then the roll of a drum at same point.

WISEA'.   Come ! The guards assemble in force. His Liege soon mounts the throne, and I who sit in the royal shadow must mount mine [depreciatingly] which be at the footstool of royalty, but the rim of his dais— There I must chatter at every opportunity like a parrot for pleasure of the Court.

Exit Wiseacre and Pauline L. hand-in-hand.

THIRD SCENE.

Scene.—Grand saloon and audience chamber in the Margrave's Palace, canopy and dais R. Three thrones upon dais. The Margrave's throne (or chair) in the middle upon a second dais. The Chamberlain, Grand Usher, Grand Judge, Lord High Coroner, Grand Commissioner, Lord Youth and a number of Courtiers, both male female, await the Margrave. They are spread about in groups, all talking in dumb show as the flats open. Two soldiers with spears, and in armor each side of arch, which is C., a pair of embroidered curtains concealing arch, before whom stand a couple of Ushers nearly elbow to elbow. Enter Wiseacre C. through A. Shoves aside Ushers and walks down stage a few paces. The Ushers shake their wands at him, replace curtain and resumes places. The Lord High Coroner, Chamberlain, Grand Judge, Grand Commissioner, Lord Youth and some Courtiers of both sex now gather around Wiseacre. All look smilingly at him except the Grand Commissioner.

LORD HIGH CORONER.   Gramercy, sir jester, right glad are we to see thee, since ye have given o'er to literature we have missed thee from our sports.

LORD YOUTH.   [Shrugging shoulders and grimacing.] Aye, marry ; how fares the tragedy ? Is the poem completed.

WISEA'.   [Bowing·] No, my gosling Lord, 'tis partly in the embryo state, and therefore resembles thee.   In other words 'tis but half finished.

Wiseacre looks stolid. Lord Youth assumes the air of one displeased, and all the Courtiers smile and look merry except the Grand Commissioner who curls his lips scornfully.

LORD HIGH COR.   My friend, if I may be so bold, what is the subject of thy poem ? The same old story I suppose—the same old tale that delights the poet and the painter.

WISEA'.   Thou art right, it be a tale of love. Yet also art thou wrong. For though love hath always been since our first parents, love ne'er grows old, else it be not love.

GRAND JUD.   Thou hast a tongue fit for diplomatist's part

WISEA'.   Yet ne'er shall it be stained in [that vile art.

LORD HIGH COR.   Ever facetious in ryhming most tellingly. By my knowledge of thee, I do assume that thy composition must be like thy converse, which I predicate hath lost none of its sparkling wit. Come, a truce with this raillery ; spout us a stanza or two of thy dramatic poem.

GRAND COMMISSIONER.   Sneeringly]. A *Fool's Play—must be a jest, forsooth.*

WISEA'.   [Bowing.] Mark well, good friends, if this Lord speaks the truth.

LORD HIGH COR.   Fall back, gentlemen, fall back your worships, give mouthing room unto our bord, your Honors.

All that have come forward retire a few paces, forming two circular groups, one R. and another L., the Jestor takes C. yet a trifle up stage facing orchestra.

WISEA'.   Ladies and gentlemen, the part I'll now narrate, is the opening passage in the 1st scene of 3d act, where Captain Leon, a sort of philosopher and warrior knight settles down and partially retires from the world, holding it somewhat in contempt· Though unacquainted with the tender passion, is taught to love on beholding the pure and regal Lady Ida. You see after beholding the noble maiden, he takes to reading tales of the heart ; she perceives that he loves her unknown to himself, and being desirous to fix her name more securely in his mind, she gives him a book to read on the fly leaf of which she hath writen a poem, making the Captain and herself the hero and heroine, hoping by this strategem to stir him more quickly to a proposal of marriage. He is seated in an easy chair in his study (which is enlivened by the rays of a curious lamp) with a book in his hand(Ida's book. He opens it to read ; his eyes fall on the poem. He recognizes the handwriting. He eagerly peruses it, then leans forward meditatively, gazing out of the window of his castle to the home of his enchantress on the opposite side of the river. Suddenly he arises and seizes his hat cloak and sword, mounts his horse and flies to the man sion of his sweetheart, into whose willing ear he whispers his deep love. I'll but speak the poem she wrote and when I've finished the work I'll read it through and through. Lady Ida's lines will enable thee to judge of my play, as the fragment is a correct sample. Hark ye ! the Captain now reads :

'Twas a fragrant summer's night,
And the stars in luminous splendor,
Didst reflect a light supremely bright,
The woodland seemed to render up
Itself to love,
And the sylvan elves in estacy were seen,
Some in merry circles
Sporting, dancing, singing on the turf of green,
Whilst others of a more romantic heart
Strolled off in loving couples
To plight again their throths, and tell
The old, yet new, story, in the dell,
Apart form listening ears,
Such was the night, a glorious period,
A time meet only for love,
When Sir Leon (the celibate) who smiled at woman's
    charms,
Walked forth to meditate.
First he thought only of the buds and flowers,
Then of mankind, the moon, world, and—
The blue sky's vaulted dome,
But finally, (with high and beating pulse),
Dreamed how beautiful were Lady Ida's eyes.

The Lord High Coroner pats Wiseacre on the back. The rest clap hands. All cry good, very fine, bravo, bravo, except the Grand Commissioner and Lord Youth

GRAND COM. [Shrugging shoulders.] Our good jester here hath always stood in high favor with the Royal family of Baden. Advantage he may take of this now since he's so great a bard. I much misgive me for the Princess ; ha! ha! ha! I fear that in some sudden attack of lunacy he'll essay to storm the Lady Louisa's heart.

WISEA. Ye popinjay, a role in which thou canst not play a part.

All laugh except the jester, Lord Youth and the Grand Commissioner.

LORD HIGH COR. (To Grand Commissioner.) Shame on thee, my Lord, for this display of spite. The jester's office hath always been respected—being licensed with full liberty of speech.

LORD Y. (Aside, to Wortenburgh.) My Lord Chamberlain, I'm of the opinion that our jester here is entirely too clever, too witty.

COUNT W. (Aside.) I think thou sayest right, Lord Youth, yet I cannot find it in my heart to bear him malice. 'Tis said he is the wisest Fool of the present age. Good Ethelbert prizes him highly. (Aloud.) Ladies and gentlemen, we may expect the Margrave now at any minute, by the right vested in me as Chamberlain, I do command order, that the coming of his liege may be received with proper dignity.

All take their prearranged places. Wiseacre seats himself in the Margrave's Throne. The Chamberlain signalizes with wand to the ushers to draw back the curtains, which they quickly do. Music, a grand march, softly, until the Margrave is announced by the Chamberlain.

COUNT W. His Most Sovereign Excellency, the Margrave.

Enter through arch: The Margrave, on the right hand of whom walks the Prime Minister. Next comes Prince Julien and the Princess Louise, who walk together and attended by two pages. The pages bear the train of the Princess. Behind these follow two heralds with trumpets, who are in turn followed by some military officers (on the staff of the Margrave), and some ladies and gentlemen of honor belonging to the National Palace. Then comes Captain Sir Albert Josephthal, leading the first half of the Margrave's Guards in fours, followed by his Lieutenant, leading the second half in fours. Boths enter with swords drawn.

The first column of the guards march down stage far enough to admit all their number. Then the second column does likewise. The Captain ordered his section to right-face. The Lieutenant commands his section to left-face. The Captain now orders his troop to forward-march. The Lieutenant does the same After they have crossed stage the Captain orders a left-face, and the Lieutenant a right-face, after which the entire troop remain motionless. The Captain and Lieutenant salute the throne, then sheathe swords. The Chamberlain takes his place on the right of the Captain of the Margrave Guards. The grand usher on the left of the Lieutenant. The Courtiers forming the Margrave's suite take up their station just above the dais on promp side, all the other courties gather in a group on O. P. side. the Lord High Coroner, Grand Judge and Grand Commissioner stand a little out from group. Prince Julien seats himself on the right hand of his father, the Princess seats herself on the left hand the Heralds each take a place back—nearly at the chairs pf the Prince and Princess ; the pages seat themselves on either side of the dait. The curtains at each arch are drawn together, ushers resume places, Margrave and Prime Minister stand before dais. The Minister of State a little back. Both survey Wiseacre, who pompously returns their looks. The orchestra plays 'til the Margrave steps back a step to speak.

MARGRAVE. I marvel.

WISEA. At what, sir?

MAR. At a fool.

WISEA. Then thou must marvel at thyself. The

law doth plainly say that he who occupies the supreme chair of state is Margrave, and as I now fulfill its spirit so must I then be. Yet as thou art out of office, I'll pity take and grant thee our jester's place, he having promoted himself.

MAR. Come, this be too huge a jest—make way, thou saucy buffoon.

WISEA. What—doth boldly, publicly spurn our Royal offer? Art not abashed by the presence of a ruler?

MAR. (To Wortenburgh.) My Lord Chamberlain, remove this magpie.

Chamberlain comes forward followed by Grand Ushers. Wiseacre arises with mock dignity waiving his sceptre.

WISEA. Stay, Sir Chamberlain, (to Margrave.) Sir, I abdicate. (Places hand on forehead.) Lost! Lost! High hopes, bright dreams—all fled me because I am a fool. (Seats himself heavily on the dais nearest the footlights, burying his face in his hands.) Gracious Heavings! gracious Heavings!

Chamberlain and grand Usher resume places. The Chancellor of State (Vallenstern) now steps upon first dais in front of the Princess. The Margrave seats himself in his throne.

MAR. (After seating.) For this same reason hath many lost before. Yet it's strange, too, for 'tis written, " A fool for luck.'

WISEA. (Looking up with a grin.) Aye, thou dost correctly quote the adage. Yet the definition in full thou hast not elucidated, but I will do it for thee: 'Tis written, "A fool for luck," its true. yet it's well understood that a lesser fool must yield to a greater. Now as thou art the biggest fool, thou art heir, of course, to better luck than me. 'Gainst a lesser fool I, myself, wouldst be most fortunate.

Now, my liege, more fully have I proven
Than thee, the good old maxim,
Of "a fool for luck.

The Margrave smiles, and gently strikes Wiseacre with his sceptre. A tittering runs throughout the Court.

MAR. (To Vallenstern.) My noble Lord Chancellor—occupying now our throne—being crowned, sceptred and clothed in the robes of our great office, we make known to thee that it's our Royal will ye now proclaim our Court is open.

CHANCELLOR. (Raising his mace.) Ladies and gentlemen, his gracious liege being seated in the chair of state, gives all ye greeting. I now declare this Regal Court open for justice, business and audience. Let all persons who have offended the laws, and who are legally ready for a hearing, be immediately produced and set before his liege.

The Chancellor now steps down from dais. Every one bows. The Captain of the Guards crosses to Lieutenant and pretends to give directions, then resumes his former station. The Lieutenant, after receiving the supposed orders of his superior, leaves the Court, quickly reappearing, accompanied by Gottlieb, Catherine, Philip, Rose, Myriam and Dr. Stern. The Lieutenant leads prisoner before the Margrave, then salutes, and resumes his former place. Music from the time the Chancellor stops speaking until the Lieutenant resumes his station. The ushers attend properly to curtains.

MAR. Though an hereditary Sovereign, Monarch over all the land of Baden, wearing about me the august dignity of Chief Magistrate, yet the Crown hath not turned my head, the purple inflated me with arrogance, nor the ermine inclined me to favor circumstance and pride. I find it, therefore, (no matter how complete hath been the trials by ministers of state, judges, commissioners, or those, who e'er they be, appointed to see the law fulfilled, not consistent with mine office as sire of a great and free people to attach my signmanual to sentences or rewards before a word I've had with each and all.

CHANC. As justice is first upon the list, those who wish for it stand forth. Also those who testify.

GRAND COM. (Steps out and bows.) My Lord Margrave, I crave first speech.

MAR. 'Tis granted.

GRAND COM. My gracious, Sovereign, and thou my good Lord Chancellor, I do accuse (taps Dr. Stern upon the shoulder) this man as having broken the statutes. As Grand Commissioner of Baden, I find him guilty of chicanery, and by the right invested in my title, have ordered the laws full force upon him. My liege. I do but wait thy signiture to give unto my action at the legal sanction necessary to its proper fulfillment.

CHANC. Prisoner answer for thyself unto the Margrave. This is the last chance thou hast to plead for mercy; or to defend thy cause.

DR. STERN. (Steps out and bows.) Thanks,

sire, thanks, my family name is Stern, my title is most
honorable, 'tis that of Doctor. Its just one year since
from my native England I here migrated, and opened
my pharmacy and chemical depot. I'm a graduated
chemist and pharmaceutist, under thy wise rule all hath
been sunshine. Chancing from my works and store
to be when the Grand Commissioner's deputy came, he
reported ill of me. Entertaining some spirit 'gainst my
house for reasons to me unknown. My liege he did
take oath I refused accounting. This brought my lord,
(the Grand Commissioner) himself unto my place. He
demanded that I should either pay the tax upon my
grant or return my privilege unto the state and suffer
fine or imprisonment, or both, at the discretion of His
Honor. I proved his deputy false and proffered him
payment, which he was about to accept, when his deputy called his attention to my sign, criticising it in a very
rough manner to his Worship (here). My lord thought
a moment and then refused to accept my payment, unless I erased from my sign the title of Doctor, which,
he said, on my part, was insolent arrogance, that the
title belonged only to the learned professions. I replied that my profession was as learned as any and vast
in its ramifications. That the proud rank of doctor was
of Eastern origin, and literally meant a man of wisdom,
a learned man, being alike the property of all professions, and that as chemistry and pharmaceutics went
hand-and-glove with the physician and surgeon (who
both wore the lofty title of doctor, and who had to
qualify themselves by no more labor and pains than it
takes in my art), I would not yield me, holding that I
had as clear a right unto the itle as any other profes-
sional or scientist. I have said, sire, I now await thy
pleasure.

MAR. Thou hast nobly spoken in thy defence, and
by the simplest, yet the wisest, law—that of common-
sense. I hold thee right.

WISEA. In other words, good knight of griping
pills and strong emetics—he means 'that he holds thee
a Stern truth.

MAR. Good Doctor, thou art acquitted. I prithe
now stand back.

DR. S. · Sire, my heart is big with gratitude.

Dr. Stern now resumes his station, first bowing to the Margrave.

MAR. My Lord Commissioner, we think thou hast swayed with too high a hand, for when the doctor proffered thee the laws just due thou didst err in not accepting it, committing thyself a misdemeanor· To us it appears thou art too quick to domineer, therefore, not the proper person to be trus;ed with power, so we conceive it. Best to remove thee. To-morrow thou canst deliver up thy seal of office to our worthy jester, whom we install in thy station as thy successor, and from all we know of him, we deem he'll prove the proper man in the proper place.

GRAND COM. Dismissed, and to be succeeded by a fool.

WISEA. Correct. Who shouldst follow an ass but a fool.

The Margrave smiles, the jester grins, and every one else laughs, save Lord Youth, the prisoners and the Grand Commissioner. The latter bows to the Margrave, then exits through arch C. Wiseacre now bows to Margrave lays down his crown and his sceptre, then strides pompously to where the Ex-Grand Cmmissioner had stood, folds his arms and assumes a lofty air ; then with a smile addresses Ethelbert.

WISEA:—

My liege, of thy choice thou'll ne'er complain,
For the office will a Wiseacre contain,
The proverb of "a fool for luck" is now unanswerably
    true,
Since it fits so neatly me and you.

MAR. Though thy poetic lines most cleverly compliment our noble selves, yet I'm sorry to say they are not in strict accord with good grammar.

WISEA. (Snapping fingers.) A fig for grammar, what's grammar to rhythm. 'Tis a poet's license to turn speech topsyturvey.

CHANC. The next who claims a right to speak will now approach the Margrave's chair.

The Lord High Coroner and the Grand Judge now both step before the Margrave.

LORD HIGH COR. Most excellent Chancellor that right I claim.

GRAND JUD. Great guardian of the throne and

state, as judge, before the coroner do I demand a hearing. What says your grace?

CHANC. This, my Lord Grrnd Judge, that as the Coroner his sittings holds ere thou as justice doth pass the sentence of the law, we (by license from the throne) grant the privilege of first speech to him, (to Coroner) proceed, therefore, most noble Lord.

LORD HIGH COR. (Bows.) Prisoner stand forth. (Myriam steps before the Margrave and curtesies.) Keep up thy heart, my child, (turns to Ethelbert bowing.) Most august Excellency, in mine inquest on the body of the Knight Sir Emil Vaidmeyer I find he came to his death through the hand of this woman, though from what I glean I recommend her to thy Royal mercy.

GRAND JUD. Your gracious liege, I differ with my lord, the Coroner, it having been proven the prisoner killed the gentleman, she's therefore answerable to the law. If your noble Excellency will refer to the revised statutes thou wilt find in Vol. 4, 3d Book, 1st chapter, 5th section, 2d paragraph, these words: If any person, male or female, commit murder they shalt pay the penalty by death. Mode—the headman's axe, unless the manner through discretionary power vested in the supreme Executive (or whoever represents him) be changed. [To Myriam.] Waste, therefore, no time in useless pleading, madame, for thou canst not escape the executioner's keen edged instrument of death. Yet if thou dost it will be but death in another form, which signifies nothing. Thou art doomed, thy life is forfeited to the law. [To Margrave.] I have discovered that this woman was wife unto the murdered man [Valdmeyer.] Yet this hath no bearing here. She has been proven guilty of his taking off; she hath a heinous crime committed, so, in the name of our dread law I demand her head.

MAR. Didst thou examine well the witnesses?

GRAND JUD. There were none, unless the Abbot of Holy Cross and his monks be accounted such. But—

CHANC. My Lord Judge, thou dost not presume to——

GRAND JUD. Hold, your grace, ye at conclusions jump. The Abbot and his brothers arrived barely before myself and followers. Not a monk beheld the deed committed. Nor did any one else that I'm aware of

Yet as she herself hath confessed to the taking off of Sir Emil, there is nothing more wanting.

CHANC.   In the same volume of which ye speak, same book, same chapter, and same section, thou wilt observe that the seventh paragraph reads thus: And be it further enacted that the Margrave or Regent (as the case may be), empowered are, according as they may deem best to change not only the mode of death, but to annul even the same, or alter to a term of imprisonment, or grant full pardon.   I, for one, crave executive clemency for this defenceless woman.   I believe her to be most foully wronged.   Sir Judge think not to outwit us by half quoting the law.

Abbot now throws aside curtains at arch, walks hastily before the Margraved glancing at Myriam as he does so   He is closely sollowed by brother Andrew.   After the Abbot and Holy Secretary have entered the ushers aftdus curtains and resume places.

ABBOT.   Right, your Grace—right, most noble Chancellor.   [Looks haughtily at judge, who returns his gaze in the same manner.]   Tis' not only the civic laws he misquotes, but also the sacred ones.

GRAND JUD.   Well, as regards my religious quotations, if they annoy that wart on the happiness of man, "The Church of State." they at least seem to please farseeing and thoughtful men.   Therefore I am content.   In defense of my stern legal front this will I say : (Though a Spaniard by birth, there's Roman blood within my veins.)   That I'd hang my own son if I found him guilty.   Sir, I am a justice, and as such I advocate justice.   If I were too ready to excuse criminals, or was any way lax in the dispensing of the statutes I would be unfit to occupy the *judge's bench*.   To me guilt clearly proven is a crime, and crime must be punished, else the law and mine office are mockeries ; rulers and courts useless things.

ABBOT.   The most useless of things are judges ; too severe in legal matters and too loose in sacred ones; too meddlesome in what concerns them not, too wise in what that they do not understand.   (The Abbot and Brother Andrew now bow to the Margrave.)   Illustrious and puisant Ethelbert, we come unushered, yet hope that to our sovereign and the Court we welcome are.

MAR.   Ye both have ever been, and ever shall be, yet, Holy Father, why hast thou come in such strange haste.

ABBOT. For mercy, sire.

GRAND JUD. What says the law? The state's great chancellor hath wrongly expounded it. This privilege, my gracious Margrave, which he asserts thou art invested with falls not to thee only when or where a well founded doubt may be entertained, a mistake in judgment proven, etc. This is the law now as it stands. The part of which he speaks does not yet take effect. Therefore the prisoner who laid Sir Emil Valdmeyer in the dust belongs to me as judge. Sire, though thou art sovereign yet doth the law outrank thee. Thou art but its chief executive, and must respect it as well as the humblest citizen. My Liege, I demand the prisoner, and to my warrant thy signmanual. [Presents a paper to Margrave.] Sign, Sire!

The Chancellor seizes the paper which the judge presents to the Margrave and turns to the sovereign in great agitation.

CHANC. Most noble Ethelbert, the prisoner hath not made her defense yet. Besides, the Abbot hath come to speak for her, too ; I know he has by the look he gave her on entering. Hear the prisoner, Sire! Hear the Abbot!

GRAND JUD. [To Vallenstern.] She hath none to make, aye, no defense at all. Did I not say she acknowledge the killing of Sir Emil? Therefore the priests cannot say aught in her favor. Stay no longer the hand of the Law by obtruding thyself before the pen of our gracious Sovereign [To Margrave.] Sign, my Lord Paramount, (to Chancellor) and do you, sir Chanceller, attest. Why my Lord Prime Minister leans so towards this criminal, and seems so greatly moved about the law being satisfied upon her person I wonder beyond measure.

MAR. Sir Judge, thou hast acknowledged that if there was a mistake in judgment proven, or if I entertained doubts, well founded, as to the executing of any person, certain privileges claimed for me by the Chancellor fell, then, to my right.

GRAND JUD. Thus have I stated it, sire, and again I say so stands the statutes.

MAR. And I say so do they not stand. For the rights thou wouldst deny me takes effect to-day—aye, this very day, such is the will of the Grand Council. of State. Even if it were otherwise 'twould matter little, for I hold thy judgment wrong, and on the best of grounds. Thou art aware, (or so should be,) that no person or persons can be punished on their own testimony without there be sufficient evidence, and of such, my Lord, thou art most wofully wanting.

GRAND JUD. Sire, the woman swears she did the deed, and if thou wilt but lend me thine ear for just one inch of time I'll give thee evidence enough to satisfy thee to the full.

CHANC. Bah! she may be mad—she may have sworn falsely to shield some unworthy member of her house. Thank Heaven our states Grand Council is composed of men of sense—men who aim to elevate the throne not to debase it. [Aside.] Where have I seen this woman's face? What is it that makes me incline so towards her? She hath a gentle exterior, yet I do observe underneath it all that bold fixedness of purpose which proclaims her not of that material which submissively endures an injury. [Aloud to Judge.] My Lord! thus do we treat thy warrant! [Tears it to pieces.] Comest thou here to check and sit in judgment on the Chief Magistrate of our land; he who is the judge of judges; to teach his Liege how to render justice? Back, I say! [Judge haughtily resumes former station.] Stand back till ye again are called! [Turns to Myriam.] Fair prisoner, our good Margrave will hear thy defense.

MYRIAM. (Courtesying to Margrave and Chancellor.) Sire, I thank thee for the boon thou hast vouchsafed me,—the right to speak in mine own behalf. Yet being guilty I have nothing much to say, unless it be, give unto the law the blood it (perhaps justly) thirsts for. The errors of a moment sometimes become the sorrows of a whole life. I once had a joyous home—a brother and fond parents, too. But a fiend in saints attire backed with etherious beauty and persuasive speech transmogrified this scene. My parents molder in their graves; my brother's remains became food for the monsters of the deep lone sea—where they were hurled after vainly striving to avenge his sister's injuries. Oh, my Liege, how once I loved the author of all this misery. He was my life—my soul—my happiness complete. And when to me his manner was changed, his love grown cold, my heart stood still within me. I plead, and did but jeers receive; first at my birth, then at my religion, and, finely, at my ruin—the which he had himself produced. He grew so to detest me that once when somewhat filled with wine, he struck me, applying to me vile epithets not fit to air before your Worshipful Liege. When I found we were not married I forced him to have another ceremony performed. He strove to make that one like the first, a mockery, but unbeknown to himself at the time, was foiled. Yet when he became aware of this he procured the proof, intending, of course, to destroy it, but fate willed that into my hands it should fall. Finding that I could expect nothing from him but hatred, I left him, swearing to be avenged. At this period of our lives we were at Rome, and whilst here he planned and nearly brought about my death. And, sire, he never knew until a few nights ago, that he had failed in carrying out his base design against my life.

As soon as I recovered from the fever brought on by my sufferings, I set about to consummate my oath. Our child (of which I have forgotten to mention) being dead—dying through receiving a blow meant for me. Oh, my dread Lord, when love turns to hate 'tis of bitterness the very essence. Sire, I make confession that it was my hand that laid Sir Emil Valdmeyer low in the dust. Yet it was before I had discovered he was my legal husband, for I, too, believed the second marriage a failure also. But I wouuld have killed him all the same if acquainted with the fact I'd been, for he made my life a wreck, ruined my happiness, stained his hands with my brother's blood, and destroyed my home. I have lived but for vengeance—fed upon the thought. It has been my companion by night and by day, sleeping or waking, it has never left me. It gave me vigor : it nerved my arm, yet now that my mission's performed my strength doth fail me. Oh, Sire, I pray that as I must answer for my bloody deed .thou'll not keep me long in waiting.

ABBOT. My Liege, she speaks the truth, yet hath she a point omitted, and that point is this : That if she had not taken his life he would, upon discovering her yet in the flesh, have killed her upon the birth of the first safe opportunity.

CHANC. (Eagerly.) Thou sayest truly, holy father. (To Margrave.) Sire, 'tis plain as A B C she was compelled to execute the deed. I find no reason why your liege should withhold clemency. My gracious Lord, I do advise your Highness that she be pardoned, her wrongs outweigh her sins, if sins they may be called.

ABBOT· Exalted Ethelbert, in coming here myself to plead before my throne, I have not come unarmed. [To Brother Andrew.] Show his liege our proofs – proofs on which we stake the propriety of our claim for mercy.

BRO' A. Illustrious sir, may it please your mightiness we—

MAR. Enough, good Brother Andrew, the words of Cadwallader, the Abbot of Holy Cross, are all sufficient with Baden. [To Myriam.] My child, for all are children of the throne—or else sire—addressed to the States' first citizen, be but a strange anomaly, I do reprieve thee. Thou art free to go. But hearken. 'Tis here in this respect, as in other monarchies, that when a person dies without an heir, the property escheats to or falls to the Crown. This being the case with the dead Sir Emil, his gold and bonds belong now to the Throne, and as I am the nation's steward, have power over all his goods and chattels, to do with as I may deem best. Of course, thy wifely claim must be liquidated to the fullest equity; yet, notwithstanding all these legal rights and profits, I divide the estate equally between thyself and the Convent of the Holy Cross.

ABBOT. (Bows.) My thanks are in my heart. My tongue cannot utter them· Sire, I'm overwhelmed.

BRO' A. (Bows). Most bountiful sovereign, may Heaven be always with thee in all thy undertakings.

MYRIAM. (Curtsies.) Thou last in thanks, thou canst count me first in loyalty. Sire, words are not adequate to express my gratitude. From the time of Sir Emil's death until this hour, I had no wish to prolong a life that had grown hateful; but now, thanks to thy munificence and mercy, a new influence steal's o'er me, I sigh to live. To live, if only to do good. Henceforth I dedicate myself to all who suffer. (Kneels.) Sire, thy hand I crave to kiss.

CHANC. My liege, Lady Valdmeyer hath done the State a service in ridding it of such a vagabond as this Sir Emil was. Men of his stamp are not only the bane of courts, but a curse to humanity.

MAR. I do agree with thee, my lord. (Arises and lifts Myriam to her feet.) Up, my daughter, this court permits not such servile homage to the chair as kneeling and hand kissing. .This be only the demand of tyrants or minds whose reach art circumscribed, and have not the proper balance. 'Tis absurd that dust should kneel to dust. I did but justice, else were I not Ethelbert the Just. Pleased am I to view the gloom receding from thy brow, and I hope in less than a year's good time to see thy lovely face beam with the smile that so enhances beauty. Furthermore, my Lady, there's men yet in Carlsruhe as comely as e'er thy base husband was, and, wearing hearts within their breasts, are worth the netting. I did a champion for thee observe here, (points with sceptre) in his Grace the Chancellor. (Seats himself.)

WISEA. (Coming forward—seizes Myriam's hand.) The Margrave's court prohibits hand-kissing, but Wiseacre's court allows it; that is, when it's the claw of a pretty bird like thee. (Kisses Myriam's hand, then turns to Margrave.) Sire, thou'lt say I'm out of character, yet this is my answer—that as I now have the right to grant licenses, I must certainly have the right to take them.

MAR. My good Wiseacre is well aware that to every rule an exception exists. Out of the love we bear the ladies, we feel it an honor to kiss their hands—in fact, 'tis a lovely fashion—a proper way of paying homage to women. 'Tis meet for a knight to so conduct himself, and here at court gatherings is a sight not strange. But enough! thou knowest as well as we all of this matter in question, and how and where we construe it right or wrong.

Wiseacre bows, and then resumes his station, receiving a contemptuous look from Lord Youth.

MAR. Lady Valdmeyer, art thou not of Jewish blood? Pray, what may have been thy ladyship's name? Hast thou any kindred living?

MYRIAM. Yes, sire, I am of Hebrew blood. As to my relatives, all art dead but one, and that one consists of an uncle, a younger and cherished uncle of my darling mother's. He was my youthful cavalier. Since my fourteenth year, I have never laid mine eyes upon his manly face. He was taken (the news we learnt by mer-

est chance) a captive by the Turks.   Five years he remained in bondage, after which period his captor died,
making him heir to his great opulence, and bestowing
on him his freedom.   He dwells in some one of our German States, holding a high place under the government.
Being but seven years my senior, he must be now just
thirty-seven.   That he sought ffor us I know full well,
for I'm confident he adored his sister.   She had been a
second mother to him; in fact, I know he loved us all.
But when he came, what did he find?   He found an
empty cottage, new made graves, and one, an outcast—
shame stamped upon the entrance porch, gaping destruction for a welcome.   I was too proud to have
claimed his protection even if I had met with him.   So
for twelve years, twelve long years, I've been a wan-
derer.

MAR.   Cheer up, my child, for the sunshine of a
happier life is about to dawn upon thee.   We shall consider it our royal duty to find thy uncle·

When Myriam speaks of her uncle being a slave among the Turks, the
Chancellor leans eagerly forward, remaining so until the Margrave finishes his
speech, then rushes to Myriam.

CHANC.   Thy maiden name,—quick—thy maiden
name.

MYRIAM.   (Looking surprised.) 'Twas Myriam
Isaacs.

CHANC. The lamb is found. I knew I'd seen thy
face before.   Lady, I am Ernest Vallenstern, thy mother's brother, I am thy uncle. (Embraces her.) Thou
art found at last!   Aside.) Thou art again in the arms
of him for whom thou wert made.   When a little girl
I loved thee, and none but thee, sweet Myriam, shall
ever call me husband.

MYRIAM.   Dear uncle, I mean dear Ernest, (for so
I always addressed thee,) I am made more than happy
in beholding thee again.   (Rests her head upon his
breast until the Margrave finishes his speech.)

MAR.   The storm cloud may gather with all its
strength, but it cannot withstand the power of bright
flashes.   See how at last in murky fragments it is dis-
pelled.   Pleased am I that that which began under the
shadow of the prison bars and the jailer's shackles bids
fair to end with no weightier chains than those of Cu-
pid's manufacture.   (To Chancellor.) As we have a
matter of some peculiarity on hand, and wishing after
our own fashion to shape its color, we relieve thy grace

for awhile of thy good office next the throne. Ye may stand apart with thy fair niece, (To Court.) Ladies and gentlemen, we pronounce all business relating to the Valdmeyer affair forever settled.

The Chancellor, Myri , The Lord High Coroner, the Abbot, Holy Secretary and Wiseacre, for ⟶ group together; all speak kindly to Myriam in dumb show.

GRAND JUD. (A little apart from group.) Lady Myriam Valdmeyer, since I be cognizant of all the facts to thy case relating, I do sincerely join with the good friends which now surround thee. in giving thanks that it hath terminated thus. (Bows.) In honest truth I say these words.

Myriam courtesies coldly to Grand Judge.

ABBOT. What a gentle shape the law assumes when it can do no harm.

GRAND JUD. Admitting this to be a fact, the church and the law twin brothers then must be.

WISEA'. Good Ethelbert, I think our noble judge hath an evil eye to Lady Valdmeyer's shekels. (To Judge.) Old ermine collar, there's not a crumb for thee; they were gobbled long ago.

GRAND JUD. Thank Heaven, Sir Wiseacre, the clothing of this court terminates forever thy prerogative to insult under the name of jesting.

WISEA. Ye will not hold so thankfully this change, when for thy numerous groceries the rate of charge I do increase for each and every license.

The Judge scowls at Wiseacre. The Margrave smiles, the Courtiers nudge one another and smile also. Lord Youth looks glum.

MAR. Gottlieb, Catherine. and Philip Montagna stand before me, and also Rose Marbury.

They all come forward; the males bow to the Margrave; females courtesy.

WISEA (To prisoners.) Build high thy hopes—the Margrave's got his hand in. There's no telling what he may do, my captive friends.

LORD Y. (Aside to Judge.) By St Mark but I fear that dragon-mouth'd clodhopper, Wiseacre, speaks discerningly. That other dregs than himself shall be thrushed upon our noble order.

GRAND JUD. Thou art more observing that I presumed thee.

LORD Y. 'Tis a shame—a bitter, burning shame.

MAR. I will now explain why I have called thee all before me. On New Years Eve, now just three

nights ago, disturbances were reported constantly.
Many arrests were made ; my son here and Philip Montagna and also Rose Marbury were of the number,
(Rose being arrested on parole).   The Chief of Police
reported these facts to the Minister of Police who in turn
reported unto me.   At first the matter I could not understand and so gave orders for arrests at random.
But at last my wayward boy made full confession,
thus giving light unto darkness.   In sifting the case
I ascertained that Gottlieb the watchman who had
my notice escaped these many years was no other
than the old hero, (at this juncture Gottlieb looks
abashed) Sergeant Montagna.   That Philip on the
night of his arrest was acting in the capacity of substitute for that father whose honorable wounds had pre-
cluded the possibility of attention in person.   That
Rose's crime was nothing more than meeting her lover
at " St Gregory's."   [Rose hangs her head and looks
shily at Philip at this juncture.]   And that she was the
daughter of brave Private Marbury, who, though he
died in battle, will live in story ; that Philip who having changed places with the Crown Prince (at the Prince's
instigation) had shown himself born the better to wear
that station than my disobedient son Julien.   Now,
Philip Montagna, as ye did so well on " New Year's
Eve " in guarding the Treasury, we invest thee with the
office of Minister of Finance, with the power to choose
who shall assist thee in thy honorable duties.   We
also create thee Prince of Heidelburg, Lord High
Constable of Baden and Member of our Privy Council.

PHILIP.   [Bows.]   Sire, I am unworthy of honors
such as these.   My Liege thou hast o'erwhelmed me.
Sir, consider me more than grateful.

MAR.   'Tis for me to judge who is worthy, and
how that worth shall be recompensed.   Sir, Ethelbert
hath rarely failed him in these particulars.   Young
friend, thy quick wit, boldness and honest heart, hath
saved not only my good name from being inscribed as
an artful abettor of evil doing, but hath placed the whole
land deeply in my debt.   Thou hast all the requisites
for power—a free and ample mind, high intelligence,
courage, a spotless character and a sympathetic soul.
Thy talents belong to the state, and if I did allow thy
merit to remain in obscurity I should to our country an
injustice do.   Thou wouldst not have me appear to the

world as either an ingrate or a jealous man.

LORD Y. Sire, this is hardly fair to raise this peasant to a station so lofty. As a noble, I protest, all the blue blood within my veins rebels at the thought that I—I the better born—must not only associate with, but pay court to this beggarly-begotten member of thy Liege's cabinet. Well, after this I shall not be surprised at anything thy noble Excellency may choose to perform.

MAR. Insolent boy, know that ye err. He's not a peasant, but a yeoman. Yet it matters little, for it's the heart and head that constitutes a man. Surely thou hast not pondered much on sacred Writ, or profited by the teachings of our Sunday-schools. Ye speak as though blue blood thrived only with the aristocrats. Thou art wildly astray. The fittest place to look for it is amongst the people. It lives only in healthy, vigorous bodies, and those thou'll find a hundred to one among our sturdy, hard-working, honest citizens. As to better born, the only individuals who can lay claim to such a distinction are they who have genius stamped upon their brows. Their minds are beacon lamps of heavenly fashioning whose oil is thought and whose light is wisdom. Their titles spring from the hand of Deity and in the ranks of honor take place before mere seals and parchment dignities. [To Philip.] Sir Philip Montagna, give no heed to the arrogant chattering of this silly courtier. And now, with all possible haste, make a Princess of thy charming Rose.

ROSE. [Courtesies.] My Liege, I thank thee for thy kind suggestion [looks archly at Philip], and for the blessings thou hast showered upon us all.

CATHERINE. [To Gottlieb.] Our Philip a Prince.

GOTTLIEB. Aye, wife, and a Cabinet Minister—a Cabinet Minister, God bless our Margrave.

Catherine and Rose now embrace Philip, who presses his lips to each of their brows.

GOTTLIEB. Sire, pardon them [pointing to Rose and Catherine. They are but weak women—their affections hath outrun their senses.

MAR. Weak, sayest thou ? They are not weak, no, sir. 'Tis strength they reveal, aye, the strength of a mother's love for her offspring—a woman's love for the man whom she hath chosen.

WISEA. Prince Philip, I fear thou art less modest than I have considered thee. Allow me to observe that the kissing of other than a lady's hand should be set apart as a sort of private festival. Poetically—thus:

This kind of kissing shouldst be done subrosa
Whene'er, it be my Lord, to Rosa done.

Ahem! But it suddenly strikes us that we are Grand Commissioner, and should therefore shun the perpe-trating of a pun or joke as readily we would the poison sold for liquor by our friend *here*, the Judge. [Draws himself up haughtily.]

The Margrave and Countess smile when Wiseacre finishes his pun on Rose's name, after he speaks of the bad liquors sold by the judge, they all take more license with their merriment. The Judge knits his brow. Lord Youth looks scornful.

LORD Y. [Aside.] Judge, I hate that Wiseacre—I hate him for being an impudent upstart—I hate him for the many stings his saucy tongue hath given me.

GRAND JUD. I do not love him much myself. By the gods but he can twist words to the cutting quality of a knife.

MAR. My Lord Chamberlain, for knightly honors wilt thou prepare.

Count Wertenburgh then whispers something to Grand Usher, who exits C. through arch. The ushers then holding aside the curtain until he returns followed by a Page. The Page bears in his arms a large cushion heavily fringed and embroidered. The Page and Grand Usher walk before the Margrave and bow. The Page places the cushion before the dais? the Page and Grand Usher bow again; the Page taking the seat formerly occupied by Wiseacre, and the Grand Usher resumes his station. Music all through this business.

COUNT W. [Bows.] My Lord, your Highness's pleasure is obeyed.

MAR. Kneeling, it hath been said, is by this court prohibited, yet there's one style permitted, and that's when knighthood is conferred. Our worthy friend, Gottlieb, will kneel therefore and so receive it.

Catherine looks delighted. Gottlieb appears amazed, then kneels slowly favoring his wounded leg. Ethelbert arises, puts aside his sceptre and draws his sword

MAR. In taking knighthood all are permitted to choose whatsoever name is most fancied. Yet knowing thou art fully satisfied I parley not. [Lays sword on Gottlieb's shoulder.] Arise, Sir Gottlieb Montagna, and be a knight, and when ye draw thy sword, let it be (as it ever has been with thee) only for justice and thy country.

The Page who brought in the cushion assists Gottlieb to his feet, and then reseats himself.

GOTTLIEB. [Bows.] Sire, thou hast been most extravagant in thy good will to my family.

The Margrave now takes a decoration from his breast, consisting of a star and pendent cross, and pins it on the bosom of Catherine.

MAR. Lady Montagna, accept this—'tis the badge of the order of St. Mary, a fitting symbol to shine upon the bosom of a virtuous wife and noble mother ; Wear it, I give it thee in gratitude ; wear it as a token of the love I bear thy house,

CATHERINE. [Courtesies.] My Liege, I am an old woman, and shall not long survive to enjoy the honors thou hast heaped upon me and mine. But the short lease of life that yet remains to me shall be spent in praying that God will spare thee to long make glad this happy land, and that my Philip shall always be worthy of the trust and confidence of your Highness.

MAR. Having Sir Gottlieb and Lady Montagna as parents, I take no thought as to Prince Philip being ought else than what he is—the noble son of a most worthy and excellent couple. Now, good friends I prithee all stand off.

All bow, then mingle with the groups formed by Myriam and her party. The Margrave, at the same time, picks up his sceptre and resumes his seat.

COUNT W. Sire, as the Princess De Albeaux and myself are reunited, and soon to join in wedlock. I request that ye accept my resignation, as we wish to spend our honeymoon abroad—in fact, to stay abroad for some considerable time, This, you see, would prevent my properly attending to my duties here. Furthermore, Lady De Albeaux is opposed to my longer being Chamberlain.

MAR. The request is granted. So the Princess is jealous ? She fear too much court is not the proper thing for Count Wortenburgh ? Well, the Chamberlain's birth is fraught with danger, for though he sails in *seas of beauty* he's sure to meet with *storms of sparkling eyes*.

COUNT W. [Bows.] Thanks, your Highness, Sire, thou art ever shrewd in sifting out a cause.

PHILIP. Deem me not bold after thy gracious treatment if I petition thee to appoint as Chamberlain my excellent friend, Leopold Stover, and in advocating him as a man (through his refinement and learning) every way calculated to fill the post most pleasing to your Highness, and creditably to Baden. As deputy to our Grand Commissioner I nominate the trusty Sergeant who made thy son, Rose Marbury and myself, prisoners at " St. Gregory's." Sire if it had not been that he was true to thee, things might have terminated not as they have.

MAR. Thou dost forget that thou art Privy Councillor, and, as such are privileged to advise. But I have no knowledge of this Stover, yet, stay—'tis enough, he is thy friend. I thank thee for preventing my o'er-looking of this Sergeant. But for him I might have gone down to my grave oblivious of thy genius. Thy remembrance of this man alone, Sir Philip, reveals thy fitness to command. Heaven be praised that fate hath watched and guarded so our interests. My Lord, the berths are theirs.

PHILIP. [Bows.] Through thy bounty, Sire, my cup is full.

PRINCE JUL. (Stepping before the Margrave.) Royal Father, a word have I to say. The trouble I have given thee I do lament, and in the name of my angel mother who now looks down with love upon her wayward son, struggling for that virtue which was her crowning wreath, I swear never to give thee cause again to complain, so long as I do live! (To Louisa.) Cousin, come here.

Louisa comes forward taking Julien's hand.

MAR. Spoken like a man.

PRINCESS LOUISA. (Aside.) Dear cousin, uncle knows all that thou wouldst say. I did acquaint him as quickly as from my side ye went. I did misgive me that the oath you made to reform might soon keep company with thy legion of broken promises. Loving thee as I do I wished to capture thee for my life's companion Thinking if once I were thy wife it would a blessing prove to thee, so when I saw thou wert really inclined to settle down I strove eagerly to bring about an immediate connection 'tween thou and I. I knew that I was not distasteful to thee, and I thank the Almighty for giving me success. Excuse the arts I used to win thy declaration, for, oh, Julien! I—I love thee— I love thee, Heaven only knows how much.

PRINCE JUL. [Eagerly aside.] Louisa, darling, thy confession delights me, for now I'm fully aware of the value of the prize the Allseeing hath blessed me with. (To Philip, aloud.) Prince Philip, I shall always refer with pleasure to the happy night when Julien of Baden first beheld the Lord of Heidelburgh.

MAR. One week from this period we appoint a feast, and call upon our good friend the Abbot of Holy Cross to tie these Gordian knots. In the mean time we will consult with our friend Duke Vallenstern, the Chancelor, how much the state can spare the Almoner, for we wish to make all hearts glad upon that day.

The *Abbot* and Chancellor both bow. Wiseacre rushes to C. of stage striking a tragic attitude.

WISEAC.—

> Since all this blood and thunder now is ended,
> And no one to the headsman's block is sended,
> I'll prove the fool I am and so have been,
> By marriage, and that with Pauline Sinn.

CURTAIN.

www.ingramcontent.com/pod-product-compliance
Lightning Source LLC
Chambersburg PA
CBHW032012010726
47493CB00007B/2362